THE NAKED TREES

Also in ACE Books

THE GREAT BETRAYAL
Michael Horbach

"A grim and brilliantly translated study of an army facing inevitable defeat . . . I recommend it to those with strong stomachs"—*Sunday Times*

THE NAKED TREES

TAGE SKOU-HANSEN

Translated from the Danish by
KATHERINE JOHN

ACE BOOKS LIMITED
BARNARD'S INN, HOLBORN, LONDON, E.C.1

Printed in England by Love & Malcomson Ltd.
London and Redhill, Surrey

1

It began one December day in 1943. I ran into Kjeld in front of the cathedral, and he asked if I'd come with him to the Beach Tavern, to the Christmas celebrations of a little students' club he had just joined. I was quite willing, and that evening we met again and took a tram out to the north end of the town.

We got off at the terminus. The night wasn't dark, but it was stormy. The wind was piercingly cold. Right away our eyes were watering, and every breath sent a chill deep into our lungs. We scurried across the highroad, and plunged into the woods to get under cover. But there was no shelter there! the wind still went right through us.

The road we were following was grey with frost and hard as iron. A little snow which had fallen earlier in the day was trying to hide in the ditch, but the wind kept scaring it up and driving it against us. It would come writhing down the path, rise in front of us in an eddy of dust and gravel, jab us spitefully in the face with hard, tiny grains, and then collapse and whirl into the rustle of dry leaves on the forest floor.

Kjeld was leaning forward with his eyes shut, and constantly bumping into me. He had turned his coat-collar up round his ears, and pulled his brown felt hat well down on his forehead. With one hand he was holding his scarf over his mouth.

'Are there any Germans in these woods?' he shouted, trying to look up.

'Not now,' I replied. 'The Pavilion's burnt down.'

At a turn in the road a clump of tall oaks gave us some protection at last, and all at once we were walking in a calm, with the gale booming high above us and the trees clashing furiously together in its wake.

Kjeld stood still. 'Wait a minute,' he said, gazing up.

The sky was overcast and starless. The beech trunks, dizzily tall and straight, were groaning and pitching rhythmically from side to side, and their tops made a distinct, restless pattern on the luminous grey ceiling.

5

Kjeld dug me in the ribs. 'What d'you think of that!' he said.

We walked on. The road took another turn downhill, and the bay rose before us as a sounding, impenetrable darkness. We could just distinguish the noise of the breakers from the noise of the gale, but only when we were right down on the cliff, where the tavern stood, could we see the white horses plunging in the black sea.

A shaded blue lamp guided us to the inn. We found the gable door and entered the cloak-room. A stone-deaf old man was sitting behind the counter, listening with his whole face. He already had a lot of coats hanging up on the inadequate rows of pegs. The inn wasn't used to much custom at this time of year, and the sight of us threw the old man into such a dither of sheer obligingness that he all but knocked his evening coffee and sugar-bowl off the counter.

Kjeld's small person beamed ever brighter with warmth and goodwill as he shed his outer garments. Everything about him was brown—his suit, his shirt, his hair, his joyful eyes, even his complexion. I stood watching him as he carefully combed his hair before the glass. His face looked big in proportion to the small, stocky figure. His features were unusually regular: so regular, in fact, that they might have struck you as a shade ordinary, if they hadn't been so animated as well.

A delicious warmth greeted us when we opened the door of the bar-room. Small groups of students were talking in undertones. There were lights only at the far end, over the bar; the room itself was in half-darkness, illumined only by the firelight, which threw long shadows across the raftered ceiling and the walls.

There was no central table. Along the wall stood separate little square tables, but they were spread with yellow cloths and blue crockery, and adorned, in honour of Christmas, with coloured hearts. Before each place was a candle in a small candlestick.

Kjeld rubbed his hands, and his eyes shone with delight. It was certainly all very cosy and appealing, after the wild winter weather.

'What d'you think of that!' he said again. 'Can't you feel it straight off? This is quite different from the big students' union, that silly debating club. Just look at this crowd.'

'They look all right,' I said. 'Whose are those two girls by the piano?'

'They're on the committee. Keep off them. But we can easily find two others. There won't be any with sweaty underarms and greasy hair, you can be sure of that. They weed those out at the interview. But can't you see they believe in something, this lot? They're frank and serious. They've got something about them.'

6

The bar-room was filling rapidly and the tables were being taken, and before long there must have been something like fifty members there. Kjeld and I retreated towards the bar. We found a vacant table in the remotest corner and sat down.

The door to the cloak-room opened for the last time, and a very slim, fair-haired girl in a plain black dress came tripping in on high heels.

'Hey!' I said, 'here's someone we know.'

'Why, it's Ingerlise!' exclaimed Kjeld, jumping up.

'Well, now we know this is an O.K. place. Is she a member, or only another guest?'

Of course Ingerlise was a member, but I had to supply the answer myself. Kjeld was already out on the floor to welcome her.

Ingerlise looked shyly and uncertainly round after their greeting, but all the good tables were full, there was no chance of squeezing in anywhere, and she reluctantly let him steer her into the corner where I was sitting. Her face fell when she spotted me.

'Have you changed your hair-style again, Ingerlise?' I said severely, keeping my seat and gaping at her shining, pale-gold hair. It was combed upwards in a style that revealed her lovely, slender neck and the equally lovely, downy hollow of her nape.

'And have you changed your shirt again, Holger?' she retorted valiantly. 'I believe you've actually had a shave as well. That must be the first time since we've been at the university. How on earth did you persuade him, Kjeld?'

Kjeld hadn't taken in a word she said. The ass was gazing in undisguised homage at her chic hair-do, and he was quite lost. It was a pity that from where he sat he couldn't see her profile. This evening her nose was a good half-inch too long.

'And how did *you* come by intellectual interests, Holger darling?' she asked. 'I'd never have dreamt of meeting you here.'

'It was just a mistake. Though I can see it's a smart place, as you patronize it. You do smell them out.'

I offered her a cigarette, and lit it. Kjeld didn't smoke. I lit the candles on the table as well, when I saw people around us had lit theirs.

Now the chairman got to his feet behind the large round committee-table opposite the fireplace, and rapped on his cup. He waited till all was silent. Quite silent. Dead silent. But just as he was finally on the point of speech, the waiter returned to the bar from serving in the back room and briskly deposited some money in the aged cash-register. As he turned the handle, the machine rang and clattered like a quartet of old Ford vans, and the till shot out with a crash. No one laughed, but there was a ripple of suppressed mirth, gradually becoming audible. Then the chairman resolutely spoke up, welcomed the members and the guests, and announced the evening's programme, which—as he put it—was less exacting than usual, to mark the imminent Christmas holiday: music, a reading of their own poems by two of the members, and a dance after tea. If people felt like dancing.

The chairman was no greenhorn to look at. He had the air of a grown man—tall, thin and straight: perhaps indeed slightly tense and rather stiff in his movements, but with the distinctive presence that denotes a free and fearless character. The eyes under his thick sandy hair and low forehead were alert and shrewd. But the finest and most noticeable thing about him was his voice, which was at once distinct and resonant; and though he was quite informal in his little opening speech his voice lost none of its authority.

'Perhaps,' he added, 'as we have guests this evening I should wind up by observing that we don't clap. After all, it's we who provide the entertainment, and we see no reason to applaud our own efforts.'

A trio now embarked on a piece of baroque music. It wasn't exactly sheer delight, I could hear that much—the co-ordination was too halting, and the 'cellist especially was too uncertain of his part.

The pianist, who led the trio, was, like the chairman, very unlike the average student in appearance, though authority wasn't the first and foremost thing he radiated. To tell the truth, you couldn't have found a queerer or more comic figure anywhere. He was gigantic and very fat, with a week's growth of black stubble on a couple of mighty double chins, and a streak of food-stains down his lapels. Unperturbed by the lock of blueblack hair that was constantly tumbling over his sweaty brow, he laboured with might and main to conduct the instruments and by facial contortion to keep them together. Now he would cock his pointed, childish little nose and shut his eyes behind the thick horn-rimmed glasses in immeasurable despair; now he would smile broadly and benignly as a moon, nodding the most ardent encouragement to his fellow-players.

And he had his reward. A confiding, relaxed feeling spread, evoked by the music in conjunction with the candlelight and the glow from the deep fireplace. The others in the room gave themselves up to it, gravely and pensively listening to the music, or listening inwardly to what the music had touched and stirred in themselves.

Suddenly the music was penetrated by the great, raging noise of the gale in the woods. I came wide awake and looked round. Ingerlise sat with her elbow on the table, prettily propping her chin on her little hand as she stared into the candlelight. Kjeld was leaning back with arms folded, looking fixedly at her hair. Beyond them, all round the room, I saw nothing but unguarded faces, to which the candles gave remote, shining eyes and the cheeks of children. I observed them one by one, and at last met the steady, scrutinizing gaze of the chairman, which had been resting on me for some time.

Who are you and what brings you here? Was there anything you heard that I didn't?

I felt caught, and looked away. There was mockery and arrogance around his small, full mouth, but in his piercing eyes mainly curiosity. What were those eyes seeking? I plucked up courage to meet them again, but the chairman was gazing past me into I knew not what. And once more the gale went raging over the house.

The trio concluded, and the listeners slowly returned to normal. There was a lighting of pipes and cigarettes, and attention shifted to the first reader: a fair, lively medical student who had stationed himself before the piano. He was obviously nervous and feeling his position acutely. His ears were flaming. What he read was light verse, on spring joy and autumn sorrow and the brevity and dubious delight of love, and his voice gained confidence and clarity as he became aware that his charming, self-mocking points were going down with this receptive audience.

The waiter didn't waste his time in the short pause after the medical student's reading. He flung himself with accumulated zest on his old rattle-trap, and the till shot out again, this time causing general hilarity.

Meanwhile a gloomy black-haired youth had got to his feet in the corner behind the committee-table. In his black-striped Clark Gable suit he would have looked the complete charmer, but for his flapping collar and ill-knotted tie. He did a lot of shuffling with his chair, which he clearly felt incommoded him. At last he picked it right up and passed it across the table to the chairman, who put it on one side. Then he took a bundle of white sheets from his brief-case and laid them on the table. A moment later he installed the brief-case on the narrow window-ledge; but after inspecting its position closely he foresaw that the blackout curtain would push it off, so he moved it experimentally to the table. But there it was obvious it was taking up too much room, so he opted at last for the floor as being in every respect the safest and fittest place, and the brief-case vanished under the table.

A girl's bell-like voice pealed with laughter at him, but the dark student remained as grave and concentrated as ever. He cleared his throat and gathered up the white sheets. At the last moment it looked as though he were going to make a preliminary remark, but he gave up the idea, reached for his glass and took

9

a gulp of water instead. Then he cleared his throat afresh and began.

He read in a dark, solemn voice, monotonously, now and then actually chanting. But though his delivery far out-soared the normal compass of everyday speech, it wasn't hollow. It was sustained by intensity and a striking emotional power. The poems dwelt chiefly on the nobility and glory of love. The longest had as its subject the will to realize the dreams of youth, the bitterness of the awakening when life's hope proved false, and the moment when happiness was revealed as—the dream of happiness.

The room was breathlessly quiet as he read. If everything up to this had been met with goodwill and sympathy, people were now straining their ears for every word. And there was no mistaking the effect. This wizard with his spell-binding stanzas was laying irresistible hold on the hearts of his audience and tuning them to his own pitch. He was filling their minds with visions and ecstasy, and it was as though youth itself were speaking, as though its exuberance and stark desire had found a tongue in his passionate verse. Poem after poem came from his wide, scornful curling lips. He read himself free of churlishness and secret distaste for his audience, but not out of his original gravity. He only once raised his head to look at the room, and that was when the waiter, who had long been shuffling his feet at the bar, thought he might exploit a break between two poems to work his cash-register: the poet paralysed the man with a brief glance from his keen little eyes, and he collapsed on a chair till the reading was over.

Just as the last poem was dying away, and before the spell could break, the fat pianist with the baby face sat down to his instrument and played without the slightest stumbling a piece by Buxtehude, thus prolonging and deepening the effect of the poems and at the same time easing the transition to informal gaiety.

Kjeld sat dumb and entranced long after the tea had been poured out. Now and then he turned his eyes with emotion to where the wizard was sitting, and seemed on the verge of rushing across to embrace him in grateful enthusiasm. Ingerlise he had completely forgotten.

But Ingerlise didn't forget him so readily.

'Your tea's getting cold, Kjeld,' she said.

Kjeld awoke with a start, and turned quickly towards her with such an overwhelmingly happy and open glance that she at once looked down at her plate. Those eyes were no good as a looking-glass.

'I feel I've had an answer,' he said at length. 'That was great, that last reading. It's like something I've felt and dreamt of, and yet haven't really dared to believe in. Now I know it's possible—it exists. And it's as if that were all I needed to know.'

I sat quiet as a mouse, like a schoolboy nervous of being called on, but Kjeld didn't ask me what I thought of the reading. Ingerlise, however, at once nodded sympathetically and felt just as he did.

Suddenly someone up at the round table burst out laughing, a peal, a roar of laughter, which increased in volume and seemed interminable. It came rolling down on the company like a landslide and within seconds had silenced all conversation. It was the wizard, throwing himself back in his chair and bellowing. An exuberant, heartfelt shout, from genuine excess of spirits, but not without malice: there was evidently a butt up there, whoever the poor devil might be.

Soon after that Kjeld got up and valiantly approached the committee-table. We saw him accost the wizard directly, and we saw the wizard lending a gracious ear and then smiling with irregular, black teeth. In the end they made room for Kjeld at the table. The chairman pulled out a chair and pushed him down on it.

So Ingerlise and I were thrown on each other's company, since Kjeld was the only member we knew. We didn't say anything. Not a word. Indeed we were both so persistently silent that it came as a relief when the lively medical student began strumming on the piano and presently struck up a dance tune. I asked Ingerlise to dance. It would pass the time.

She was light as a feather against my hand, and her perfume was deliciously cool and a little heady. 'Ain't she sweet', went the music, and involuntarily I held her a little closer. But the rhythm was too quick. It wasn't with me she should be dancing this tune.

I noticed what a lady she looked here, with her new hair-style. The other girls weren't ladies, they were just grown-up girls with something gentle and chubby-faced about them, an only half-conscious femininity: each an unassuming little flower that could be content to grow unheeded in a corner, until one fine day when she would overwhelm with unsuspected sweetness the man who lit upon her, and come suddenly into bright and fragrant bloom. But with Ingerlise, everything was calculated. She had never been a real small-town girl.

'I've often wondered what holds you and Kjeld together,' she said, when a slower dance-number began. 'I can't make out your relationship.'

'It's quite simple. We've been friends since we were boys.'

'I know *that*. But I sometimes feel positively frightened when I see you together.'

'Frightened?'

11

'Yes, frightened that you'll do him harm, because you don't understand him. And because you can always find out people's weak points.'

'Well, as a matter of fact I've often saved him from a licking. He was horribly cheeky and fond of teasing when he was small.'

'He's so alive and warm. And cheerful and impulsive.'

'And eager and spontaneous and frank and sweet.'

'You're not to poke fun. Kjeld believes in something, he believes in a great many things. But what about you? Do you believe in anything at all but yourself?'

'Not that I know of. Heaven forbid.'

'Of course not. I needn't have asked. It's impossible to imagine a greater contrast than you two. Really, I feel like separating you.'

'Have a try, then. But first tell me when you became such a fan of Kjeld's. At school you thought him rather a nuisance with his eternal adoration, if I remember rightly.'

'That's none of your business!' snapped Ingerlise. 'Besides, Kjeld's developed a lot this last year,' she went on more pleasantly.

'And he seems to be making some smart acquaintances at the moment,' I said, looking across to the corner where Kjeld finally showed signs of getting up.

Ingerlise did not deign to reply, but the dance ended at last, and the happy Kjeld made his way to us and took his beloved by the arm. I could withdraw with a clear conscience and settle down to observe them.

A handsome couple they were. And not only performing in dashing style, but able to keep a conversation going as they danced. Very impressive. Was this affair really coming to something at long last? If so, I could soon write off my friendship with Kjeld. Anyway, as things looked now they'd be spending the rest of the evening on the dance-floor.

I was just going to order myself a beer, though apparently it wasn't done to drink anything but tea here, and was already looking forward to hearing the cash-register again, when someone behind me laid a hand on my shoulder. I turned round, and there was Frederick—Dr Ove Frederiksen—standing behind me, with his big, genial frog-face all of a twitch. My last underground contact, whom I had thought safe in Sweden.

'What on earth are you doing here?' I exclaimed in bewilderment.

'It's surely for me to ask that,' said Frederiksen, smiling till his eyes were lost in the crinkles. 'I'm a member, which is certainly more than you are. I hope you're enjoying yourself!'

'Shut up,' I said. 'Have you been here all evening?'

'I've only just come. I've brought my wife. May I sit down?'

12

He settled himself in Kjeld's chair, and we began swapping news over a couple of lagers.

'So Svend Åge didn't talk after all,' I said. 'Where is he now?'

'In the camp at Frøslev. Till further notice.'

'Are you back at the hospital?'

'Oh, yes,' he nodded. 'But who do you think sends his regards? Who do you think I've just seen? Leo. Old Leo.'

'Where? You can't have. I was over at the garage asking for him only yesterday.'

'Well, you can't have been there today; because he was there today, and he was very impatient. But of course we're cleaned out now. We've got to start all over again.'

Frederiksen yawned wholeheartedly, and gently stroked his face as though to smooth out its innumerable wrinkles. He was short of at least forty-eight hours' sleep.

'Then is it to be papers again?' I asked.

'For me, yes. But the rest of you might look out for something a bit stiffer, don't you think?'

We had another beer on the strength of the unexpected meeting. Before he went back to his wife, Frederiksen told me that one of the best friends of his student days, a Copenhagen fellow who was now a doctor himself, was coming to take up a hospital appointment in the new year. A man with useful experience, and someone with certain contacts to build on. We settled that I should look in on Frederiksen two days after Christmas.

When it was time to go, I went off with Kjeld and Ingerlise. The wind had if anything increased. Over the water lay a great bank of greyish-black snowclouds, but just above us the sky was clear, and there was a cold, hard twinkling of little stars among the bare, restless trees. Kjeld stood slightly apart, gazing upwards and possibly thinking himself unobserved.

'What a lot of stars are out now,' said Ingerlise, taking his arm. 'So long as they don't get blown down!'

'On a night like this, one has cosmic perceptions,' said Kjeld. 'One can actually feel that we live on a floating globe whirling along through space, don't you agree?'

'Ooh, yes,' said Ingerlise. 'But do let's walk on now. I'm freezing.'

We followed the path by the water, inland to the dark town. The gale boomed on through the woods, and the breakers beat and beat against the cliff. Kjeld and Ingerlise were confidentially discussing poetry, as far as the wind would let them, and I was thinking about Leo, back at last.

2

A JANUARY morning, and the new year's raw, sober sun. Snow
had been tumbling down over the town all night; now it was
peacefully melting in the streets, and the day was still and mild.
Trams were clanging their patient, toilsome way between long
lines of snow-clearers doggedly at work on the roads and pave-
ments; the scraping and rattling of shovels filled the soft, damp
air everywhere.

On the south side of the roofs, where the sun was warmest,
the snow had already begun to slide off. Here and there a brisk
little woman hurrying through her shopping would be oddly
startled when it landed smack in front of her on the pavement.
She would screw up her eyes against the glare and raise them
coquettishly as she walked on, slower than before, and when the
next slide came rustling down the roof she would stop in time,
her winter-pale cheeks dimpling.

The staircase of 21 Røndevej rang like a bathroom and was
bright yellow and contemporary, just as you would expect in
the town's latest and dearest block of flats. For some reason
the name-plate inside the door had been removed, and out of
sheer curiosity I ignored the lift and walked up. The marbled
stone stair made the shaft re-echo with the respectable vacuity
if you so much as cleared your throat.

It was by no means just anyone who lived behind the tasteful
teak doors. All the way up it was the most expensive newly
married daughters and most coddled sons-in-law of the well-to-
do, and you would never have thought an outsider stood much
chance of getting a flat here among the elect. Not, at any rate,
without local influence. But who could tell—perhaps he *had* local
influence, even if he was from Copenhagen.

Fifth floor, on the right. On the door, where the former
tenant's name-plate had been, was tacked a visiting card in-
scribed: CHRISTIAN BORCK, M.D.

The bell rang noisily in an empty-sounding hall. 'Just a
moment!' cried someone inside. Then there were brisk footsteps,

14

and the door opened on a rather tall though not very robust young man of twenty-seven or twenty-eight. He had a look of firmness and character. He wore a dazzling white shirt, was newly shaved and groomed, and smelt very faintly of scent.

He stood gaping at me, his blue eyes round as marbles, but before I could open my mouth his face cleared.

'Ah, now I know who you are!' he exclaimed joyfully. 'Come in and take off your things. I'm delighted to see you.'

He shook me cordially by the hand, led me into the hall and relieved me of my wind-jacket.

'How peaceful it must be round here, for you to be at large! If I were the Gestapo I'd arrest you on sight.'

I suppose I smiled dutifully but none the less he was rather shocked at his own quip, and hastened to explain how glad he was to see me and what a good thing it was that I'd lost no time.

'We'd better use first names right off,' he added. 'It makes things easier.'

He laughed again, and opened the sitting-room door, with a flood of animated apologies because the flat was still in a mess. It was only a day or two since he'd moved in.

For the first few minutes all I saw was the view. Facing south-east there was a huge oblong window nearly the width of the wall. I encountered a dazzle of white light from the snow-clad, sun-bathed uplands of Mols and Helgenæs. The air was so clear that I could see deep into that domed landscape on the other side. The low farmhouses, hugging the earth, weighed down by snow, leapt to the eye. There a mill rose up, there a church spire pointed into the air. I saw what seemed a black ant moving across the snow: it was a lorry toiling on its belly over the crest of a hill. Straight opposite was the bay, a sheet of gleaming, dead-calm water. On the other side I could just distinguish the black, sloping wintry woods of Marselisborg. In the foreground, almost at my feet, lay the harbour with its silos and cranes and coal bunkers, its long jetties and wharves and ships' funnels.

'Do sit down,' said Christian Borck. 'No, not there, for heaven's sake! That chair got a crack in the spine when we were moving. Take the other one. And here's some tobacco,' he added, putting a big wooden jar on the table. 'It's a bit damp, because I've poured some rum in; otherwise it's unsmokeable, that stuff.'

The room seemed very stylishly furnished. A bookcase, a fine old bureau, a grandfather clock, a mahogany table combined with modern, uncomfortable chairs. On the walls were engravings of old Denmark as a prehistoric, wrinkled, crumpled embryo. I could see, next door, in a small room giving on to the balcony, a painting and the end of a divan. I saw nothing of the mess the host had apologized for.

'Strictly speaking I should live in,' Christian said, 'but the hospital quarters are so deadly dreary. Besides, they're too small —I just couldn't have got my things in. So I fixed this up. It's essential to have a decent place, don't you think? And then there are other reasons why it may be convenient for me to live in the town.'

'Yes, Frederiksen told me——' I began.

'I know all about that.' Christian jumped up from the sofa and began walking to and fro. In passing he snatched an apple from a bowl on the mahogany table and devoured it at incredible speed.

'Personally I haven't much faith in this idea that the invasion may come in North Jutland and so we've only to build up as many fighting groups as we possibly can. After all, it would be pretty silly of them to try and land here, wouldn't it? Whereas we know definitely that the Swedish transit has been stopped, and that all German convoys from Norway will be crossing Jutland. So although reserve groups and illegal newspapers may be all well and good and have their usefulness, we must above all and as soon as possible be in position to cut the railway lines whenever we choose. *That's* the job. At least that's the only way I can see it.'

He stopped before the mahogany table and looked critically at the apples in the bowl. Suddenly a fretful quiver twitched his eyelid. He took out a handkerchief and carefully wiped his mouth. Then he lit a cigarette and went on.

'So we must hurry and get a few sabotage groups formed. If there are others in the town doing the same we'll meet up all right, but as yet we don't know. And for the moment we've nothing to work with either. No arms, no explosives, no manpower—it's all as pitiful as can be, and we don't even know when we shall get anything. In all modesty, I've had some experience in Copenhagen, I belonged to a group over there, so I can at least teach you the elements. But there must be several of us to start with. How about that?'

'We've got Leo,' I said. 'He's worth two.'

'Indeed?' He smiled. 'You mention him with reverence. So he's a dyed-in-the-wool bloodhound?'

'He's a mechanic, and he's been a corporal in the army,' I said.

Christian nodded appreciatively. 'How did you come across him exactly?'

'We happened to be sitting next each other at a big Nazi meeting—a long time ago now. First off I thought him a loathsome fellow, I assumed he was a Nazi, and of course he was thinking the same of me. But as soon as the speeches began he started making a row, and in the end both of us were thrown out.'

Christian went over to the window and stood there half turned

16

away, so that I couldn't see his face. I gave an account of the joint achievements of Leo and myself: not that there was anything to brag of—they were soon reviewed. Our organized 'official' work had consisted in perpetually dodging round with a duplicator, distributing illegal newspapers, and raising money by private contributions. On our own initiative we had got hold of a pistol each by attacking two lecherous German soldiers in Lovers' Lane. Not very heroic, since they both had girls in their laps, but there! On the other hand, there was hardly any ammunition for the pistols. Then Leo had concocted some incendiaries—petrol in a beer-bottle, wrapped up in rags well soaked in petrol and turpentine, and a thin little bag of phosphorus round the neck: a kind of Molotov cocktail—and by this means we set fire to a German pub in the middle of the town. Unluckily it was only the fittings that got wiped out, because some idiot called the fire brigade. Things went a lot better next time. We broke into a small joiner's shop in one of the suburbs, got the floor well dowsed and put a match to it. There were heaps of lovely shavings out there, and they caught like thunder and lightning. It made a terrific blaze, and we felt quite proud of ourselves next day when we heard the building had been burnt to the ground.

There was nothing else worth mentioning. I said no more, and Christian Borck didn't turn round. He had obviously calmed down, by the window. Before, he had seemed—not exactly agitated, but perhaps a little fidgety. He was strikingly active and energetic, and from the start there had been something enviably uninhibited, buoyant and direct in his manner. Plainly he was accustomed to meeting with no opposition.

He was smoking and looking down at the harbour. Or was he? Was he listening to me? Was he bored? Or was he so quick in the uptake that he could listen and think of something else at the same time?

It was soon clear that he had been marking my words. As though slightly impatient, but still without looking at me, he said: 'And then what?'

'I don't think there's really anything else worth mentioning,' I replied.

'Do you really not think so?' he said slowly. 'Wasn't there something about a repair shop where Leo had been employed?'

So he had talked the whole thing over with Frederiksen. He knew every detail in advance, but it pleased him to put me on trial. Now he was watching indifferently a little cargo-boat outward bound, gliding noiselessly through the still, black water of the harbour, scarcely a touch of foam at its bow.

That workshop was rather a sorry business: Frederiksen had been very angry when he found out that Leo and I were respon-

17

sible. But we had promised to mend our ways, and that had been that; and in any case it had nothing to do with Christian Borck of Copenhagen.

'We thought the man was a collaborator,' I said curtly.

'Did Leo think so? Wasn't it rather more of a private vendetta where he was concerned? If you're to be quite honest?'

'The man was a Nazi and an exceptionally stupid brute,' I said. 'And if he wasn't a collaborator then, he is now.'

Dr Christian Borck turned at last, and looked at me sharply.

'I hope you realize you'll both be fired on the spot if there are any more of those capers,' he said gravely. 'For the present you're to do nothing whatever on your own account, you and Leo. Don't you see that you might wreck our whole prestige with your hooliganism?'

I said 'Oh,' and there was a silence. The cargo-boat had passed the long, snow-covered outer mole. It moved out of the harbour and set course southward. Now the engine was going full out, and smoke poured from the funnel and hung low over the shining water.

'Be as angry as you like,' Christian went on. 'But it's immensely important that we should get hold of the right people at the start. Later there may not be much time to sort out recruits, but the core we're forming now must be sound. And if you knew how few there are of us you would be appalled and lose heart. But just because we're so few, the spirit of the individual counts for a lot. That's obvious, surely?'

He sat down opposite me on the sofa, and passed a hand through his curly, colourless hair. A disapproving spasm twitched his eyelid again. I noticed now that all his features were slightly blunt, the nose a little too short, the mouth a little too small, the cheek-bones and the square forehead far from perfect.

'We mustn't delude ourselves,' he said. 'Not even now in 1944 can we count on the support from the people that they're always talking about. The people——' He snorted at the word. 'The people are with us today and against us tomorrow. In the long run they're on the side of the biggest tobacco ration, we know that much. If the country's to be saved, it's up to a small number of individuals, a mere fraction of the whole. And there's nothing strange about that: it's always so in critical situations. But the men we employ must realize that the struggle for freedom is something serious and not a boy's prank. They must regard it as a personal concern. They must embody the values we're fighting for, be the living incarnation of them, so to speak. Perhaps you think it sounds odd, but,' he said urgently, searching for the right words, 'this is what I mean: we want those who—feel a liability for the whole; who—make no distinction between the fate of the country and their own fate.'

18

'If it's to be such a choice company,' I said, 'Leo and I had better back out at once and set up on our own.'

Christian looked at me blankly for a moment; then a fiery flush spread over his cheeks.

I said: 'I think all that sounds a bit pharisaical, if it's to be taken literally.'

'If it's to be taken literally!'

'Yes. The less solemn one feels about underground work, the better it is in practice. If you had to think of all that, you'd be a nervous wreck every time you saw a German soldier.'

'Will you stop acting the fool!' said Christian indignantly. 'You understand me perfectly well. Do you think I don't know who you are?'

'At least,' I retorted, 'you've made a thorough investigation of me.'

'And you think that was only because an idiot from Copenhagen wanted to lord it over you!'

'If I'm to be quite honest—yes; or something of that sort.'

'You're right. You're so right. You're nothing if not versatile. I hope you felt at home at that Christmas party. I know where you were.'

'Naturally. I beg your pardon for not reporting it, but I'm still considering whether to join the club. It was very interesting the other night.'

'Yes, wasn't it?' he said ironically—though he wasn't an ironist at all, but a puritan. 'With the enemy in the country, the brave little band of the elect gather round candles and read poems to one another. Oh, how well I know it! It's the usual thing here. For goodness' sake don't imagine that kind of club has anything extraordinary about it. There's a thriving crop of them at the moment. All over the place they're sitting with unquenchable candles, peering at their souls. Now, when reality is on top of us and nobody has to dream it up.'

'They must need a doctor,' I said. 'The age's idol in the white coat.'

'You're very witty,' he snapped. 'And I'm an absolute fool, blurting out my ludicrous worries to people who can't even be bothered listening. All right, let me go on being a fool and confess I'm worried. I'm afraid there are too few of us after all, and that we can't make it. That we're already finished as a nation. I know quite well that's a notion no one will thank me for. But I come of an old family, the last in an endless line of steadfast tin soldiers, and I can't cure myself of thinking in nations, even if it *is* out of date. I should have been killed in South Jutland with the rest. Invasion Day was the last chance for my kind, that's obvious.'

By now he was fairly trembling with excitement, and my

19

conscience smote me for having needled him. Vexed at his weakness, he jumped up and started pacing the floor again. He tried to laugh and pass it all off, but the laugh didn't sound right. It came out as a sincere, almost hysterical little outburst of despair, and some of my liking for him came back.

'Don't misunderstand me,' he resumed, when he had his voice under control. 'I don't look down on adventurers, as long as they're not braggarts. They can be better company, and above all pluckier, than most people; and if they know the risk and mean to pay for their fun, then there's more in them than mere love of adventure. You can tell Leo from me that I look forward to meeting him. I don't look down on him. The only people who get my back up are those who think it beneath them to join in. Often they're the very ones we could use. But they're so damned clever, so thoroughly *au fait* with these struggles for freedom. They've read them up—after all it's not the first time in history that a country's been occupied—and they know in advance how it all comes out, and that *we're* going to win. I'm blest if they don't think it a shade vulgar of us to have picked the right side, and they actually try to find excuses for the Germans.'

He was getting violently worked up, obviously speaking from bitter personal experience. But I listened now with only half an ear, for someone had inserted a key in the front door and was blundering about in the hall and putting something down with a bump. Christian had heard nothing, or at least gave no sign of it, and went steadily on with what he was saying.

All of a sudden the sitting-room door flew open, and a young woman in a mouse-grey coat blazed before us. She pulled off her gloves and the black alpine cap she was wearing, and shook out her dark hair.

'I thought as much,' she said with a caustic smile. 'I rather thought I could hear someone exercising the hobby-horse.' She gave me her hand. 'How do you do,' she said. 'I'm married to that gentleman.' She nodded at Christian.

'Yes, this is Gerda, who has done me the honour to become my wife,' said Christian.

It had never occurred to me that Christian might have a wife, and certainly not a wife like this. She wasn't a bit refined-looking. Her face was round and robust, and so coarse-featured that she looked all but common. It wasn't the thick, jet-black eyebrows that did it, nor the hair, cut short and also looking black at first glance though in fact only a very dark brown. It was the eyes. They were small and narrow, so that you couldn't rightly catch their expression. And it was the mouth, which was short, and full, and could express a good deal.

She and Christian exchanged some practical remarks on her purchases, and touched on various other acquisitions called for by the move and the new flat. Christian did the talking, and it was obviously also he who made the decisions, while his wife just stood there with her full lips and narrowed eyes, looking sulky. But there could be no doubt that she was the stronger of the two, and for a moment I even had the feeling that Christian was rather scared of her.

Mrs Borck started shuffling the apples in the fruit-bowl when her husband seemed to have got through his memorandum.

'By the way, those are wretched apples you bought,' he said.

'Aren't they?' she replied pertly. 'But now I suppose you want lunch?'

'You'll stay to lunch, won't you, Holger?' asked Christian. 'I've got quite a bit to do today, I'm due in the ward at one o'clock.'

I knew by his tone of voice that he would really prefer me to say no thank you. But after all we hadn't got down to business, and besides the situation was really too tempting: so I said yes thank you.

The lady of the house turned her back and vanished as startlingly as she had appeared, leaving the room dead. Christian said nothing, I said nothing. It was the old clock that finally broke the silence: it sighed audibly, collecting itself for its asthmatic, dull, noonday strokes.

How on earth had an idealist like Christian come to marry a girl like that? How had he dared? For those few minutes she was in the room she had been present so intensely that she might have scared any man, even one who wasn't born yesterday. She was certainly a living incarnation, as Christian required people to be, but what radiated from her was no very choice selection of human values. It was defiance, and independence, and what lay beyond—indifference. She was ownerless. Nobody's girl; not Christian's wife, not so bound here that she might not walk out any minute and for good.

Christian didn't try to revert to our doctrinaire discussion. He dwelt on the formation of the group from a less abstruse angle, meanwhile drifting uneasily about the room.

From the kitchen came the crash of a saucepan lid falling. But that was only a soft prelude to what followed. In the next few minutes the noise from there increased steadily. Never can female have clattered so remorselessly in a kitchen to produce a bit of lunch. What a row she made. Lids slammed, pans overturned, china rattled, knives and forks shot to the floor, taps coughed. But it went too far: gradually it was obvious that it couldn't be mere clumsiness, still less nervousness or unquenchable vitality—it was a deliberate childish demonstration, rough teasing executed with relish.

Christian couldn't take it at all. That was written all over his face. The nervous quivering of the eyelids came back, in both eyes this time, and wouldn't go. He noticed it himself and tried in vain to control it. Valiantly, with an ever more suffering expression, he ignored his wife's clatter and went on talking to me: but he was forced to give up in the end.

From the kitchen there came now a long-drawn-out wailing. Mrs Borck had burst into song. She sang like a kitchen-maid, in romantic, melodramatic style, and poor Christian abandoned all further attempt to speak. In his distress he turned to his cherished heirloom. Cautiously undoing the door of the faithful old clock, he wound it up and sedulously adjusted the hands. He took a long, long time over it. It was a kind of exercise in self-control.

But even though Christian was now silent and his wife fairly wallowing in utterance, I couldn't make out what she was singing. To judge by the tune, it was a rather vulgar ballad about sinful love and cruel death, but I failed to catch the words. Nor did it help when the kettle began whistling out there and was left to whistle away while she wailed on.

Just as the situation was becoming absolutely impossible, Mrs Borck switched off the kettle, and with that her song stopped abruptly. The door was kicked open, and in she came: quite unconcerned, with the most nonchalant air in the world, smartly swinging an overloaded tray on to the table in the little balcony-room. Not a teaspoon trembled.

Christian immediately closed the door and set about laying the table. A moment later his wife reappeared with a bottle of schnapps and three small glasses. But by now Christian was equal to her.

'Splendid!' he exclaimed. 'That's just what we need. Now we can drink to the invasion and the new year.'

And so we did. We drank to the Allied landing, and to one another. But the atmosphere at table was undeniably rather glum. Gerda didn't utter a word, and Christian's conversation was so conventional that I blushed for him. So there was only one thing for it.

'Do tell me,' I said to Gerda, 'what was that you were singing out in the kitchen?'

For a moment she seemed to contemplate a denial that she had been singing. Then, as she finished a mouthful, she said: 'It was German. South German. My husband loves everything German. But unfortunately I can't sing it in here. He says it's not house-trained.'

'I can't think where she gets hold of those ghastly songs,' said Christian with an embarrassed smile. 'They always occur to her when I'm having a serious discussion in the next room. I don't know why it is.'

'There's nothing odd about it,' Gerda replied. 'You inspire me. Simple.'

'You two seem to have a lot of fun,' I said. 'How long have you been married?'

'Thirty years this summer,' said Gerda, putting the point of her knife in her mouth.

'Nearly two years,' said Christian correctly, relieved that I had made so light of the performance.

Still, it was quite a pleasant meal. Gerda seemed to have no great interest in what we were talking about—she minded her plate and her glass and became slightly withdrawn when she had satisfied her hunger ; but she did no more demonstrating. And her face had changed imperceptibly: it was now more personal—not so featureless, as it were. There was more in it, after all, than defiance and sarcasm. Once as she was handing me a dish across the table I met her eyes and they were no longer small and screwed up. They were open and quite calm, and I saw the colour of them. They were a soothing grey.

As we sat round the table and I had time to observe them together, their marriage seemed less preposterous than it had seemed at first. I even made a kind of sense out of Christian's choosing her. It was of course on grounds of racial hygiene. He wanted to get new blood into his effete old family, so that there might be more of them to defend their country on sterling principles. But if he had thought this girl was going to let herself be refined and made over as a matter of course, he must certainly be having to think again. At any rate she was putting up some resistance to the educational process, though perhaps only because he had gone rather too idealistically and untenderly to work. But whatever the situation was, it was no concern of mine.

At ten minutes to one Christian and I went down in the lift and walked out into the high, clear winter day with slightly spinning heads. The air felt a little colder now, and we swung along by the man-high piles of already dirty snow at the edge of the pavement, full of spirits and energy. I saw him right to the hospital.

3

CHRISTIAN had asked me to get hold of another man, so that there would be four of us at least in the group. I had named three prospects as being likely material and pretty sure to come in, and he had subjected me to a real third-degree examination on their personal qualities. Finally he numbered the candidates, telling me to approach them in that order, and on no account to put any pressure on them. These suggestions were what we had been discussing while his wife racketed in the kitchen, and while we were eating lunch.

Quite rightly, his first choice was Ejgil—a thoughtful, quiet fellow whom no devil would suspect of breaking the law: on the surface lazy and not giving a damn, in fact an imperviously stubborn individualist, who in great and small things went his own way and never lost sight of his objective. It was Leo who had discovered him. Like Leo he was a skilled mechanic, and one day when we had too many illegal newspapers to dispose of, it occurred to him that that stiff-necked camel he had served his apprenticeship with might be up our street. It turned out that he was, and Ejgil was soon one of our principal distributors. At the technical college where he was studying engineering he could get rid of as many copies as we liked. He had only to be a quarter of an hour early in the morning and dump a pile in each classroom. Quite simple ; but we were impressed by his cheek, for at that time we were still running up and down staircases and sticking the papers through the letter-boxes one by one. Ejgil wouldn't put up with that at all. He used his brains, and hit on a better way.

The day after my visit to Christian I looked up Ejgil. He lived with his parents—or to be exact, with his mother. His father had been arrested by the Germans quite unexpectedly. They came for him one autumn day at his place of work—he worked for a big factory as a driver. The affair was somewhat mysterious. No one could make out why they wanted him: he wasn't up to

24

anything, and he knew absolutely nothing of importance. It was Ejgil's rule never to talk at home. But the old man couldn't keep quiet ; he was in the habit of bestowing his candid opinion on anyone who would lend an ear. This lack of discretion, though in itself harmless, had most likely gained him a number of ill-wishers in the course of time, and the chances were that one of these secret enemies had informed against him. When he had been inside for a month the Gestapo had to let the case drop ; but instead of releasing him they had sent him to the camp at Frøslev—no doubt for impertinence.

It was in a sooty and dismal tenement near the station that the family had their home. The murky, mildewed stairs reeked of cabbage. In the blue paint daubed over the window-panes as a blackout, children and errand-boys scratched smut and drew obscene figures, as though in a public lavatory. The caretaker painted them over time and again, but they reappeared at once: the same drawings in exactly the same places, like a sorcerer's formula.

Ejgil himself opened the door. Deathly pale as usual. He always looked as though his lungs were riddled with tuberculosis.

I knew at a glance that I had come at the wrong moment. Though I had brought nothing to hand over, as I usually did, of course he was aware of what I wanted ; the sight of me embarrassed him and he was at his wits' end when I asked if he had time for a talk.

Voices were audible in the flat behind. Many voices. There was a mutter as of several conversations going on at once, and a streak of blue cigar-smoke came drifting under the sleepy, yellow hanging-lamp in the hall. Some sort of family council. Today was clearly no good.

'I can come back tomorrow,' I said, and was about to make off.

All this time I had had the feeling—I don't know why that his mother was listening to us behind the door ; and sure enough she suddenly bobbed up, shoved Ejgil aside, and filled the whole doorway.

A tall, heavy woman in a vast grey apron. Worn with toil and worry. Cowed by grief and hopelessness. The moment I saw her face it flashed on me what might have happened, but it was too late then.

She looked me over with pale, watery little eyes. Then she said, without a greeting, without any preface at all: 'I'm Ejgil's mother. Our dad's just died in the German concentration camp. We heard this morning.'

She spoke quite low. With the quiet, inalienable authority of the lost. Like someone at the bottom, conscious of safety, because at last there's no farther to fall.

'So now you've come for my son,' she said.

25

'No, ma'am,' I replied quickly, 'you're mistaken. I have nothing to do with the Germans, and I'm very sorry——'

'Am I mistaken?' she broke in wonderingly, and as though waking up. Then suddenly she was all there, and her voice burned with resentment. 'I want none of your quibbling,' she said indignantly. 'Do you think I can't see what you're after? Maybe you don't know who you are? Then I'll tell you straight. You're Old Nick himself. At any rate he sent you here!'

Ejgil had been nervously shuffling his feet in the rear. Now he laid a hand on her arm and tried to push his way past her.

'There, Mum, that's enough,' he pleaded. 'He couldn't know, could he? Leave us to settle it ourselves.'

The big woman lowered her eyes. She turned to her son, her expression softening as she looked at him. Ejgil changed into a very small boy under her gaze.

'You?' she said. 'You're staying here!'

And in a rough, clumsy gesture, which might have been either a caress or a blow, her big paw swept across the back of his head. Then, without another glance at me, she took a step backwards and slammed the door.

I went down the stairs and out into the street, found my bicycle, and rode off.

The weather had turned frosty again. Even here, in the centre of the town, the east wind had lost none of its piercing, bitter cold, which could get at you however far you crept into yourself. Under the low, stormy sky with its riot of clouds the world was ice-grey and desolate. The puny trees along the cylists' path, now slippery as glass, were no longer alive; they were present only in shape, frozen to the marrow, rigid as sticks which the gale might snap any minute.

I had no thought for where I was going. The bicycle headed south of its own accord, out of the town: and that was the right way, for I was going to Kjeld now. Of course. Out to the yellow villa with the peeling walls where I had sought refuge in the past.

As soon as I remembered that house, the vast, timeless rustling of the summer trees began sounding in my ears. The beeches at the edge of the woods behind with their long-drawn roar, the light birches and swaying poplars round the deep, mossy lawns, were incessantly repeating: Come, man, forget, forget! Everything passes, but here we have plenty and don't care!

That long sough in the tree-tops and the sound of laughter. For beneath those lordly trees flourished a family life that was anything but melancholy. All the year round, the dilapidated villa rang with laughter and gaiety. Here they had no secrets from one another, and here, if anywhere, you saw what it meant to have a good time. Sheltered by bountiful parents and given every encouragement, the four children of the house had grown up, always free to follow their inspirations of the moment. The girls played and sang, danced, drew and painted, and it was all just for the joy of it, an impromptu without the faintest hankering after a professional career. Though they had talent, each in her own line, they never bothered to keep things up, but quickly dropped them for some new fancy which they were no less welcome to indulge. In the end you felt not so much that they were making too little of such good conditions as that they came by everything too easily.

For anyone who had grown up in a less ideal milieu, there were incredible scenes to be witnessed in that happy house—on winter days, for example, when there was a birthday party and the family staged their original comedies in the puppet theatre for the children's guests; or it might be any day at the dinner-table, where parents and children discussed common concerns on an equal footing and carried new purchases and changes in the housekeeping by a majority vote.

It was the father, the wispy little barrister all but hidden behind his horn-rimmed glasses, who acted as chairman. He was the smallest of the family and the only quiet one, the least noticeable, yet the most important in a way, since he was the one whose ant-like labour and self-denial provided the wherewithal to keep the household going. The first time I heard his voice was at dinner. While for once the children were all holding their tongues at the same time, he gazed raptly at his gentle golden-brown lady, whose beauty, for him, had retained all the glowing enchantment of youth.

'What are you looking at?' she asked, noticing his intentness.

'At your wonderful eyes!'

He said it slowly, clearly, and with deep feeling. And his proud lady, lowering her eyes of vernal blue, laid her hand on his.

It was truly edifying to hear—for they were both about fifty at the time, and the children sitting round, with no attention to spare from their plates for such an everyday matter as their father's demonstrativeness, were practically grown up.

All that was years ago now. The three girls married young and left home, there was hardly a year between the weddings; and suddenly the glorious laughter had died away and stillness entered the yellow villa. The only one left was little brother Kjeld, the straggler, the idol and special pet of parents and sisters. He was at the university now, but exactly what he was studying his parents did not inquire, so long as he was willing to live at home with them; and indeed Kjeld had yet to decide what he meant to be when he grew up.

I had not rung up in advance—as I usually did when going to see Kjeld, so as not to have the long ride for nothing—and when

27

I got there I had the feeling, for the second time that day, of being in the way. Kjeld was at home, but he seemed, for once, busily employed, and greeted me with a comically determined look on his chubby face.

We went straight upstairs and settled ourselves in his spacious room. Up there it was a real retreat. From the deep, worn easy chairs nothing could be seen of the outer world but the sky and the tops of the dizzily tall, shifting poplars at the foot of the garden. It was his father's study Kjeld had moved into, the only spot in the house that had been from time immemorial a haunt of silence and concentration. And today surely there was more to it than the overwhelming number of books, the thick carpet covering the whole floor, and the noiseless alarm-clock. I could see that Kjeld had something definite on his mind.

Tea was brought up. There were home-made cakes with it, and a bowl of fruit and nuts—left over from Christmas, which lingered on warm and fragrant in the corners of the house. We had not seen each other since that evening before Christmas at the Beach Tavern, and I was expecting Kjeld to revert to it right away. But curiously enough he didn't. Instead he talked diffusely about his three sisters, who with their husbands had been home over the holiday. He struck me as perhaps rather absent-minded, and slightly graver than usual; but even so, I shrank from wrecking our mood of intimacy and kept putting off what I had really come for.

However, there was no getting out of it, and at last I screwed myself up and began telling him of the scene I had just had with Ejgil's mother, back in the town. Before I got half-way through I regretted having started. The room turned so unpleasantly quiet. Besides the resistance within me, I had to overcome a resistance in the very atmosphere, or so I felt. In the end I was stranded deep, deep in my being, as if very drunk. The room had receded; I saw it fading away, far, far off, as through an inverted telescope, while my unsteady voice laboured on about things that couldn't possibly concern this place.

Kjeld sat there impassive, grave as a judge, gazing down with a set expression at his green carpet. And I knew all at once that it wasn't an attitude of distaste. He wasn't shutting me out, he was just failing to understand me. He simply couldn't grasp what he was being told. The experience I wanted to share with him remained on my hands. And I wished, I wished—but too late again.

It was only when I stopped talking that I heard how the elder-branches were chafing each other and squeaking in the wind. There was one particular branch that scraped languidly against the wall whenever a gust swept round the house.

28

'Now look here!' Kjeld suddenly raised his head and shook off his gravity. 'Just why are you telling me this story?'

'For fun, of course. Don't you think it's amusing?'

'Are you meaning me to volunteer instead of the man you didn't get?' he asked, unperturbed.

'In a way, yes,' I admitted. 'Sorry to have been so long-winded about it. I came to ask if you'll join us.'

'How strange that you should come *now*,' Kjeld burst out, smiling to himself. 'A month ago, even a fortnight ago, I'd have been sure to say yes. I can't see what there was to prevent me. Today I must not only refuse, but I must ask to be spared the illegal papers you've given me now and then.'

'So what alters the case is that meeting we were at before Christmas,' I suggested, meaning to short-circuit him and exploit his own surprise tactics.

'Got it!' returned Kjeld eagerly. He wasn't a bit unprepared; on the contrary, all his enthusiasm broke free now he had reached his own ground. 'I think I've made something out, you see. I think I've discovered myself. Who I really am, and what I'm to do in life. At any rate, it's as though my life had all of a sudden found a direction and a goal, where before I was only a sample of anonymous youth.'

'Whereas from now on, for a change, you'll be firmly resolved to mind your own business. News at last!'

'In the right sense, that's absolutely it,' he laughed. 'I proclaim a state of emergency. By which I certainly don't mean what you do.'

'How is it to be taken, then?' I asked.

'I'll tell you!' Kjeld straightened up and sat right forward on the edge of his chair. 'The thing is, while I was listening to them out there at the tavern, it occurred to me that I—— No,' he broke off, confused and blushing, 'never mind that It's all so new to me. I prefer merely to say that I believe in personal vocation. That certain people, at any rate, have a vocation in life, and that it's our duty, the duty of such people I mean, to accept their vocation and try to follow it. Then if they feel that some day they'll be able to shoulder a great task, they must preserve themselves till they're strong enough to do it.'

'Relying on the anonymous idiots to sort things out for the moment,' I put in.

'What do you mean by that?' he said, floundering.

'That there's a war on.'

'Ah, yes!' He recovered his balance. 'I quite understand the temptation presented by the war. When one's got as far in civilization as we have, as far from the elementary, it's quite natural to believe that one's outlook may be purified by going to war.'

'No!' I said.

'No? I don't believe it either. On the contrary, I believe each one of us must try to preserve his individuality and live as personal a life as he can.'

'Build up inner preparedness and thereby prevent disasters,' I finished. 'Not counting those that have already happened.'

'No, no,' he said. 'It has nothing to do with politics. I'm not interested is politics, you know that. It goes far deeper. What I mean is that there's any amount of physical courage in the world, there are crowds of people who'll go to their death by order. But how many are there who die for a personal conviction, a hard-won faith? How many have the moral courage *not* to die, to complete a personal development and remain themselves?'

'In this country,' I said, 'they're still the vast majority. You can set your mind at rest.'

'Do you really think so? Do you believe, for instance, that the majority of our classmates feel they have any obligation to themselves? Not they! They resign themselves to the formula, the sooner the better. If a conflict arises in their minds, they act their way through instead of suffering their way through. They react against it instead of shouldering the pain of being undelivered. If they're anxious or madly impatient they immediately grab at something concrete—a car, a motor bike, a bottle, a revolver—no matter what, as long as it doesn't hurt *them*. Sooner smash up the world! Don't you think I'm right? You bet I am! For now, at our age, is just the time when it's settled whether a man's to abandon himself and become a print of his surroundings and nothing more, or whether he's to break through to an original form of life. Do you see what I mean?'

'I know it by heart. ". . . In these days, so momentous for our country, the population must conduct itself with sobriety and obey the King's call of April 9th for peace and order",' I quoted.

'Yes. What I'm saying has actually never been more to the point,' he said firmly, looking me straight in the face. 'Can't you see that? How can anyone stand war and join in murder and assault, destruction and sabotage, except by getting outside himself? And why should anyone plunge into that kind of thing unless he wanted to escape from himself? I don't know what I'm supposed to say to that story you were telling me, but I can't understand its not shaking your confidence a little.'

'Why should it? I can easily find someone ready to help us out of this temporary little difficulty.'

'This temporary little difficulty.' He threw me a scandalized look, then gave a short laugh. 'Why, that's exactly right. You lay claim to human lives for the sake of a temporary difficulty. I just can't imagine how it must feel, going from door to door like that.'

'No need to make such a thing of it,' I said lightly. 'It was damned bad luck, but what else? I don't see how I could have avoided it, nor can I see that it proves anything whatever.'

'The story may not prove anything, but at least one can't help wondering whether all these democrats and dictators have ever done any good to simple people like those you were after today. I'll tell you what—frankly, I should say they were quite justified in throwing you out. For God knows whether the two sides fighting for the world now will seem very different in twenty years' time. When all's said and done they're out for the same thing—power, and only power. Otherwise they wouldn't have been so equal. And that's just what makes it absurd to have all this sacrifice, voluntary or not. Don't you agree?'

He gave me no time to answer—and indeed what could I have said to that last observation?—but got up and crossed to the window. Outside, the winter day was growing dark, but I could see how the gale was bullying the distracted poplars at the foot of the garden. Kjeld pulled down the blind, drew the curtain with a jerk and switched the lights on. Enough of that. Anyway we shouldn't quarrel.

'To change the subject,' I said, 'how is Ingerlise? I take it you're seeing each other, now you've decided to reconstruct your life?'

'Indeed we are,' said Kjeld, pleased. 'In fact she's coming to dinner this evening, to meet my parents."

'Well, well! It was nice of you to tell me, I'll be off in good time.'

'I didn't mean it like that,' said Kjeld in dismay. 'You're very welcome to stay!'

'I know that. It's entirely on my own account I'll make tracks. I'm afraid things are going too fast with the pair of you for me to keep up. In a moment you'll be telling me you've already slept with her.'

Kjeld went copper-coloured with bashfulness and umbrage, the pure soul! For him the other sex was indeed holy. At the age of seven he was a woman-hater, and at fourteen he blushed when he saw a lady's bicycle.

'Need you be so crude when you know how I feel about her?' he said in a hurt voice.

'You're a good old platonist, you are, but isn't it about time you grew up?'

'Do you never stop thinking about girls? Is there never anything else in your head?'

'Indeed yes. Weren't we just talking of the war?'

Then a great light dawned on Kjeld. I could actually see his face brightening, illumined by a sudden, overwhelmingly plausible connection of ideas.

'Now I see what it was she meant!' he shot out.

31

He had to get on his feet, to stand up and take a turn about the room so that the thought could have a good stretch in his short body, so fully was he possessed by his new insight. 'Of course! Why, it's as clear as day!' he said aloud to himself several times.

'If it relates to my humble self, I might have a first-hand suggestion to offer,' I said discreetly.

'I should think it does!' returned Kjeld with glee, catching sight of me in the chair.

And now he apostrophized me—eager, insistent, yet withal objective, as though his remarks stemmed from some lofty and impersonal apprehension of truth, which must surely give me the highest and most disinterested pleasure.

'Now I'll tell you. It's strange you should never have thought of it yourself, for they're two sides of the same thing! It's the same craving for annihilation and extinction that drives you to underground work and to all those girls of yours. You should keep off them, you should really!'

'Well, I've tried, you know,' I said humbly. 'But it made me so dizzy. One gets such a beastly buzzing in the ears. Haven't you noticed?'

But the fight was lost, and there was no time to win a new one. Kjeld had *seen* me. I could feel almost physically how he was now dissociating himself from me, and how, minute by minute, we were getting farther apart.

'Oh, stop talking nonsense,' he said patronizingly, and there was a wholly novel assurance in his voice. 'You see, the fact is that you're after one thing only—to be knocked out. If you have to stand up and think for long at a time, it starts you panicking. You turn desperate, you have to get out and fight and find someone to knock you down. Don't you think that's so?'

'No doubt. But if you'll take my advice, keep off Ingerlise. There may well be passion in her, but it isn't erotic; it's social ambition.'

'Or spiritual ambition!' Kjeld corrected me sharply. 'And that's just what I need. I long to be seen and understood as I really am. Ingerlise never casts suspicion on me, she believes everything I say to her. She's beyond comparison the most intelligent and sensitive girl I've ever met.'

'I've never said she was stupid. She's a great illusionist. In her you always see yourself as you imagine yourself to be. She can reflect your being precisely as you'd wish it to look. And that's all she can do. There's no independent nature in her.'

'So she's perfectly right about that too!' Kjeld exulted.

It was really fascinating how it all worked out. Everything I said to upset him merely confirmed his diagnosis. I couldn't get through to him any more.

'Right about what?' I said fretfully.

'She says you hate her, and have persecuted her ever since she—well, because she once refused you——'

'Refused what?'

'You must remember quite well. Of course for you women can't be human beings, they simply have to be animals.'

'In love affairs it is a regrettable fact that the majority of normal men cannot permanently ignore fulfilment,' I said didactically. 'Therefore one should, unless one is made of blotting-paper, keep clear of Ingerlise and her like. She'll lead you up the garden path, let me tell you. Just mark my words! And anyway I prefer not to meet her ladyship here.'

I rose to go, and he didn't detain me. But he saw me out, and indeed all the way to the gate. He never stopped talking. He was very friendly, and more than friendly: he was tremendously cordial and solicitous, as one can be when one feels decidedly superior to somebody.

His pride was excusable. First he had discovered himself, then he had affirmed and demonstrated his independence to an old friend, who had always sat on him, always been the stronger and the cleverer and the one who took the decisions. From now on he was free, marvellously free. I couldn't grudge him his triumph.

Yet we stood there by the gate in the icy, windy evening, and couldn't quite take leave of each other. Kjeld was shivering uncontrollably. He had no coat on.

'You should see if you can't make it up, you and Ingerlise,' he said encouragingly.

But it was a conventional remark, he didn't mean it, and I said nothing in reply. I mounted my bicycle and shook hands.

On the way home I was cursing Ingerlise. Not only had she carried out her threat of trying to separate Kjeld and me, but she had got a good deal farther with her project than I would ever have believed possible. The friendship between Kjeld and me was no recent one; it had begun when we were eleven or twelve, in boyhood's unswervingly faithful 'middle ages'. It might have weakened now that our interests were so divergent; for the last few years the bond might have existed chiefly by virtue of what it used to mean; it might well be that even friendships ought to be reviewed on occasion and not maintained at all costs. But that a girl like Ingerlise should bring about this review in our case enraged me.

B.

4

WHOM did we get as a fourth in Christian's group when Ejgil was prevented and Kjeld refused? We got Jakob. A crofter's son studying theology. A real ploughboy-student to look at. Long as a pole, thin and bony. His large hands and feet proclaimed him a country boy, like the signs of toil that marked his whole stooping figure. Jakob had put in a stint at home before he was kept at his books. He was no sprinter. On the pavement he remained stiff and slow, but for toughness and endurance he had no equal; and to see him charge across a ploughed field!—there he felt at home.

However, the fact that he had been only third choice on Christian's list had nothing to do with his clumsiness or with any other physical deficiency. It had to do with a point of inscrutable darkness in his character. Jakob was prone to queer turns. Incalculable urges were astir in his soul, and they were apt to find rather odd expression, making him a bit of a joke in the college where he lived.

For the most part he attended doggedly and conscientiously to his work. Day by day he could be seen shambling off to lectures, absent and self-communing, with centre-parted hair always unkempt and ragged and flopping on his temples, and long, crooked arms dangling at his sides. But he had been known to stall on the way to a class. He would stop dead, as though struck by an invisible hand, to plumb the depths of his lanky soul. Then after a time passers-by would see him turn resolutely on his heel and steer a purposeful course for the next dairy, and ten minutes later he was to be found in the college kitchen with a pound of butter and a very small white loaf, busily engaged in carving first the butter and then the loaf into slices, the same number of each. With the strict butter ration of those days, it was a full couple of months' allowance Jakob was thus squandering. When he had finished cutting he carefully assembled the slices—drew them up in a fine, straight row. Then he started on their consumption from one end, and, his countenance gradually becoming quite transfigured, ate his way unrestrainedly through this festal meal. White bread and butter. The Fathers of the Church couldn't have beaten that.

Whether Jakob's gluttony had any deeper source than malnutrition and a sudden fondness for himself, or whether his freaks were really a substitute for more perilous promptings, he had this slightly disquieting way of going off into trances and awaking to sudden, apparently irresponsible decisions. He would lose himself, just where he stood, in goodness knows what ruminations; but that he hadn't vanished into sheer luxurious self-forgetfulness was evident from the way he came to—it had the stamp of panic.

I've seen him run amok in a cinema queue. He had been standing beside me mute and peaceable, and we were nearly up to the ticket-hatch, when suddenly he awoke and saw where he was. Shut in a low room, encircled and crowded by people on all sides. His face was distorted by terror. With a demented gleam in his wide eyes, he gored his way through the wall of humanity like a mad bull and was gone.

Of course his conduct might have the simple explanation that he was a stranger in a town and found it hard to get used to so many people, but still there was a grain of lunacy in him. His erratic, desultory form of consciousness made him too easy to surprise and stampede, and you couldn't feel sure of his immediate reaction in a crisis. What he did might just as well be calamitous as dead right: hence Christian's misgivings.

Jakob had no misgivings; he was all for being a saboteur, however little he might know of himself in general. I arrived to find him alone in his college room. He was sitting in the middle of the floor, the exact centre, straddling his great long legs as he cleaned out the bore of the unserviceable old shotgun which normally decorated the wall over his bed. He had cleared the desk of books and other irrelevancies, so that he could put down the spare parts of the gun as he finished cleaning them.

'Still no papers?' he asked, raising his narrow face with the deep-set eyes.

'We're going on to rougher stuff,' I replied.

'Well, now!' smiled Jakob, squinting down the barrel of his gun. 'Sure you've the nerve? It was touch and go whether I'd come back here after the Christmas holidays. They're doing something about it back home, you know. Whereas what are we doing here?'

There was no call for abstract, idealistic, ethical deliberation. In his own way, Jakob had a sense of reality. He at once asked when he would be getting something to shoot with, and I was reckless enough to promise that he should soon have the chance to clean and assemble a modern weapon, which was likely to

35

be far less impressive but on the other hand far less innocuous than his own old cannon.

So our group was formed, and just a week after my visit to Christian we all assembled for the first time in the flat in Røndevej. It was not without qualms that I went to that meeting. Leo and Jakob knew each other in advance, though only slightly; but how would Christian's choice furniture accord with them? Leo was far from devoid of social prejudice—the most ordinary politeness would affect him like a challenge; and Jakob was too much of a provincial to back up a superior Copenhagen type off-hand. They might both simply dig in their heels.

And Christian. Would he for his part manage to accept us without obvious condescension? How were we going to live up to the standards he set for defenders of their country? As to what might happen if he began giving patriotic and moral lectures to Leo and Jakob as he had to me—I preferred not to think of that.

In the end it all went unbelievably well, and I might have spared myself my anxiety. Leo and Jakob were alike open and confiding, and Christian never so much as glanced at a dogmatic theoretical consideration. He got straight down to an account of the underground work he had done in Copenhagen and simply gave us all his concrete, practical experience unabridged. It was exciting and instructive, the cream being, of course, the actions themselves, which he took us through in every detail, with paper and pencil at hand to sketch the trickiest situations.

How that man could present a subject! It was a display of really brilliant gifts, fired by the eager questions that Leo, especially, put in time and again. What descriptive power, what breadth of view, what lucidity and technical grasp! And technical competence was just what Leo and Jakob could appreciate. The fact that Christian's knowledge was accurate and detailed wherever they were able to test it by their own experience inclined them more than anything else to believe in him even when they had no means of checking. He won their loyalty and attachment long before the evening was over, and became our leader in more than name.

Christian had planned another couple of meetings for our instruction in the use of various firearms, and of course above all in the use of explosives, but unfortunately he had to give up his idea for the simple reason that he could get neither arms nor explosives to demonstrate with. As yet there was no contact whatever with any of the distributing groups we knew to be active around the neighbouring towns, and I gathered from Christian that the immediate outlook was not too bright. But though in the circumstances instruction was rather a lost cause, that didn't mean we had to waste time. There was still plenty to get on with.

Between us we nosed out certain likely objects of sabotage in the city, and Christian selected three of the most practicable and assigned them to us. Jakob and Leo each got a workshop, and I a small factory. Our task was now to spy out these three places and to collect, within the next week, all the data that would permit the concerns in question to be closed down in a becoming manner.

Was the factory turning out anything essential to the war? How many men did it employ? Was it working day and night, and if so, when did the shifts change over? If there were sabotage guards, how many were there, and what was the drill? And then the matter of access itself: how did one get into the area, where were the telephones, what about the get-away, who lived in the neighbourhood? How many men did the action require? As far as possible we were to get information by the use of our eyes alone, for of course it would look suspicious if we asked a lot of questions.

Leo came out top in the first round. He had missed only one thing, namely the harmless little fact that his workshop was doing nothing at all for the Germans. Christian, however, very kindly abstained from making an issue of this little oversight. On the other hand, the reports from Jakob and me were found wanting. Then Christian said two pairs of eyes were better than one, and made us change places so that in the next week Jakob was on my factory and I on his workshop. Christian's method of grilling you was so close and searching that it brought out just what could safely be inferred from your observations, and above all what couldn't.

We continued the game with fresh material, and were soon equal to the problems that Christian set. Yet he never praised us; nor did he ever repeat anything he had once expounded in detail, and we had no idea whether he was pleased with us or not. He usually sat there with his absent, indifferent look, as though he were thinking of other things or listening to himself. But of course that was just when his attention was keenest, as I had been taught once and for all.

Several weeks passed like that, and we learned to move about the town with eyes in the back of our heads. We kept a close watch on the movements of the Germans, especially their convoys in the harbour and railway yards, and what we saw we reported to Christian, together with our proposals for action. To start with he rejected them all, but as time went by without a sign of either arms or explosives, he was more and more often obliged to fall in with our ideas, if only to keep us up to the mark. When Christian took a proposal seriously, he always set

37

the whole group on it; some he looked into for himself, and thus we found ourselves with a number of approved and fully planned acts of sabotage, highly suitable for beginners, but still without so much as a grain of dry powder.

February passed, and half March. The time could no longer be spun out. Patience had long since gone, we were sick of running about the town to no purpose, and all four of us were getting pretty depressed, when at length, one memorable day, an innocent-looking suitcase appeared in the cloak-room of the main station. Not because we had got a share in a local distribution. The suitcase was from Copenhagen. Christian had gone to work personally, and asked his old group to spare us a little something.

In the suitcase were eight small half-pound packets of the English plastic explosive PE2, which we used ever after, a roll of Cordtex fuse, containers, detonators, and five explosive pencils. It wouldn't run to more than a couple of modest actions, three at the outside, yet we felt ourselves in clover. Now at last the first small blows would be struck.

I have never had the 'underground feeling' so sharply as that first time we were out: the impression—no, the certainty—that everybody I met could see at a glance what I was up to. We had been waiting so long in mounting impatience, we were so familiar with the idea of what was now at last to be done and so burning with desire to do it, that it must, I felt, be legible in our faces, and I couldn't make out why no one stopped us, why no one ran to a telephone booth to call the police and the Germans.

The action itself could hardly have been simpler. We had chosen a small boat-repair shop, well tucked away in a back-yard in Finlandsgade. It was working day and night, but there were no sabotage guards, and towards nightfall there was apparently not a living soul around, except the ten men working on repairs to two German speedboats.

But one important point about the operation was not clear. We had no idea how we were to get in to the boats, for the door would most certainly be locked and barred; but when we put the difficulty to Christian, he waved it aside with the remark that we must just leave that to him.

We worked out a neat concentrating movement, though in this instance concentration became rather theoretical, since there was no need to go so cautiously to work. At precisely half past eight we were at our posts: Jakob at the nearest corner, Leo and I in our respective doorways opposite the gate leading into the work-shop. Leo, as arranged, had found an excuse to enter the yard, and made sure that all was normal. All three of us were armed, Leo and I with our German service pistols, Jakob with Christian's Colt, which he had borrowed for the occasion.

The street was empty, the evening dark and still. It wasn't raining, but whether it was warm or cold I can't say. I was sweating with suspense. My heart was thumping till I could hardly breathe, my mouth was dry, I had an aching void under my ribs, and telling myself not to be such an ass didn't help very much.

Fortunately we hadn't long to wait. Quick steps sounded on the flagstones up at the far end of the street. Light though they were, they re-echoed noisily between the low, black houses. A gentleman impeccably dressed in a light-coloured raincoat, grey felt hat and gloves was coming towards us. He had a black brief-case under his arm.

When he was all but abreast of us he looked up and made certain we were where we should be. Then he turned in at the gate and disappeared. Leo and I hurried across the street, and Jakob left his corner and started moving in our direction.

Christian waited in the yard till Leo and I came up with him. Then he went briskly across to the workshop and knocked hard on the double door. Leo and I sneaked over to the wall and crouched down under the window. The blackout curtain didn't quite meet the frame, and a thin streak of light shone down on the uneven paving. There was a man standing right against the window. He gave a snort of annoyance at Christian's knock. Then he laid down a heavy spanner and trudged across to the door.

'Who's that?' he called out in a squeaky, ill-humoured voice. 'We don't let anyone in at night!'

'No, I should think not, the way things are,' replied Christian in his most winning tones. He spoke very loud and clear. 'But I wonder if you'd be so kind as to tell me whether you have a Mr Ove Petersen here? There's an important message I have to give him.'

'*Ove* Petersen?' asked the voice. 'No, we've nobody by that name. *Ove* Petersen? No. It wouldn't be *Otto* Petersen you mean?'

'Oh, I beg your pardon!' Christian exclaimed in annoyance. 'What am I talking about? *Otto* Petersen, of course, I suppose I couldn't just have a word with Otto Petersen at the door? You needn't open up.'

'I'm afraid he's not here tonight,' the voice behind the door squeaked regretfully. 'He's on sick leave till the end of the week.'

'Oh, how annoying!' Christian burst out with genuine irritation.

A stream of oaths came whistling by my ear. It was Leo swearing between his teeth. We hugged the wall closer and held our breath, while the workman fought a short battle with himself. Then curiosity got the upper hand.

'His brother-in-law's here,' came the voice haltingly, hopefully. 'Do you want to speak to him instead?'

'Oh, thank you! Yes indeed! If it's not too much trouble. It'll only take a moment,' Christian replied. We could hear a smile in his voice.

'We're not in such a damned hurry,' cackled the man, well satisfied with himself and starting to tussle with the bolt.

'Bjarne! Just give Bjarne a shout,' he called over his shoulder.

Christian stepped back a pace, and made us a mocking bow as the door swung open. After you, gentlemen! Whereupon Leo and I charged in, pointing our pistols at the men and bellowing down the workshop: 'Hands up!'

My voice cracked with nervousness, but Leo gave them a terrific bawling-out. Obviously he hadn't been a corporal in the army for nothing. But you could tell that he too was nervous. His blistering oaths were to cover up his qualms.

The little doorkeeper got a shock, and the workmen were badly scared as well. It didn't take many minutes to round them up. Naturally they were allowed to get their coats and personal belongings, and after that they were handed straight over to Jakob, who was in the yard, herding them down to the shelter.

But two young workmen in the rear had grasped what was happening and couldn't quite bring themselves to walk out; they couldn't take their eyes off Christian and his brief-case. Christian had addressed himself right away to the speedboats, and after giving the engines a look over he began to unpack. As he was fastidiously drawing off his gloves and laying them aside on the planing-bench, the two inquisitive workmen caught his eye. To our astonishment, he threw them his best smile and beckoned them over—and proceeded quietly and charmingly to explain what he had in mind. Step by step. He showed them whereabouts in the engine he meant to place the charges—and they confirmed by nods that he had found just where it was most vulnerable; he demonstrated how he would secure the two small packets with a bit of insulating tape, and connect them with the fast-burning white fuse, so that they might go off simultaneously, and he held up the explosive pencil.

'In this explosive pencil—it really does look like a metal propelling pencil, doesn't it?—up at this end here there's a small glass phial with acid in it. When I squeeze the outside cap—it's made of copper so it's quite soft—the phial breaks, and the acid eats through a little wire, which releases a sparking-pin, which comes down on a priming, which transmits the spark to the detonator itself. There are explosive pencils with all sorts of combustion periods,' he explained. 'From five minutes up to twenty-four hours. This one's for ten minutes, you can tell by the colour of that safety-pin there. It's black: if the pencil had had an ignition time of half an hour, it would have been red.'

The whole display lasted only a couple of minutes, but that was long enough for Leo and me, who in the meantime, feverish and butter-fingered, had set to work on the other engine and were doing very little but get in each other's way.

When Christian himself was through, he inspected our work and lent a hand, but by that time I was already out in the yard to give Jakob the all-clear. A moment later Christian and Leo came out, and without undue haste we parted and left the scene. Two and two we went our separate ways back to our bicycles and rode off.

What sensations we had in the next few minutes, riding back through the town, and listening! The cinemas were just emptying after the first house, and people came lurching out, half-blind and bemused. Small match-flames broke out everywhere in the darkness as cigarettes were lit; and as the men slowly came round and saw the world assuming its well-known dreary contours, they reached for their womenfolk and trudged off with them. Home to coffee, home to bed. Maybe just home to the street-corner. All of them, men and women, looked strangely solitary and shut in, and none measured up to the dreams of his or her nearest. Even the couples walking along most fondly entwined were mute and alien to each other. They were still separately enfolded in the hero's or heroine's absolute embrace, staring in front of them with empty eyes and bitter mouths. How irretrievably people were walled up in themselves.

'Look at them, dumb as hell!' burst out Leo contemptuously. 'They don't know a thing, they've no idea it's us.'

How are they supposed to know? I might have asked. But Leo's feeling corresponded to my own. It was comic and grotesque that people should be walking along the pavement cheek by jowl with us—you could put out a hand and touch them—embroidering on those glossy, ever-changing film pictures, yet too dull to imagine the truth in its simplicity. They would never find us out. Never. If we only had enough cheek, which meant if we just behaved quite simply and naturally, the most incredible things could pass unchallenged. Why, the same action that betrayed and delivered while it was merely brewing, protected like a mask the moment it was done. Could it really be that the more you acted, the more invisible—and freer—you became? Then what was there that mightn't safely be done in the end?

This giddy freedom was for us—as opposed to all other people, who were outside it and could be mystified and hoodwinked unawares. For a moment I felt a spark of pity, but for a moment only.

41

'Damn it all!' Leo flared up irritably as we reached the market-place. The big vein that ran from the bridge of his nose to the hair-line on his forehead had begun to swell. 'They're not working! I told him those fuses——'

With that they worked. *Runng!* we heard. And again *Runng!* Two tremendous explosions, only seconds apart, rolled over the town, surging through every street and lane, battering on all doors and windows, drowning all other sounds on earth. Grand, grand! These first modest charges thundered like a threat and a pledge: the town shall be ours!

Leo let out a piercing whistle and leapt gleefully on his bike. Laughing exultantly, we turned off the main street into the alleys behind the cathedral. We were going up to Christian's to celebrate the occasion. What else? We could afford to take that much risk, after our first regular act of sabotage. Christian himself had invited us, in the event that all went according to plan.

It was Gerda, for a change, who let us in when we reached the fifth floor in Røndevej. We hadn't seen much of her. She always disappeared into the bedroom on our arrival, and if she did happen to be around, she never spoke. Taciturn, but as vital as when I first saw her, and growing more spontaneous in her taciturnity and less and less defiant in manner. This evening she actually smiled at us.

'So it came off,' she said amiably.

She was in a jade-green dress with a yellow apron over it and looked positively domestic and cosy. A little slimmer than usual, a little more compliant; a little more ordinary, as she went to and fro between the kitchen and the small living-room, laying the table.

Soon afterwards Christian turned up, and finally Jakob, loaded with curiosity. He wanted an immediate report of what he had been unable to see and hear, and above all he wanted to know how Christian had got the workshop door open. Leo readily enacted the whole scene for him.

'*Ove* Petersen? It wouldn't be *Otto* Petersen you mean? I'm afraid he's not here tonight. He's on sick leave till the end of the week,' he piped in the old workman's voice—duly adding the pause which had brought the tension to a climax. 'But his brother-in-law's here. Will you speak to him instead?'

Jakob keeled over backwards, rapturously displaying his long yellow teeth.

'Slick as be damned!' he crowed.

'We used that trick once or twice in Copenhagen,' explained Christian. 'It's a sure thing, if you have faith in it. There's always somebody called Petersen, Hansen, Jensen or Nielsen in a shop like that, isn't there? So you've only to add a first name. That's what inspires confidence, and gives you a chance to talk yourself out of it if you've guessed wrong. But really people are so inquisitive and so touchingly kind, they're more than ready to help you out.'

They helped Christian, at any rate. The trick was quite in his style. It was true that people gladly did him a good turn, they were delighted when he troubled them. Significantly enough, it was on Leo and me that the workmen had turned in their wrath; their manner to Christian—the one who had hoaxed them, after all—was polite, even respectful. There was one who touched his cap to him on the way out, into the bargain. Christian was throwing them out of a job, but what a pleasant man he was.

Leo had grasped that.

'You can get anything out of people, Christian,' he said. 'You've only to say to one of your patients: "Dear Mrs Andersen, I'm in such a fix! Here I am short of a real human head for some very important experiments tomorrow morning." And straight off the old girl says to you, "Eh, Doctor, if there's no one handier you're right welcome to mine. A wee thing like that! Can I just send a line to the old man?"'

Christian smiled, and Jakob asked for his dialogue with the workman over again. Leo was quite ready, and the tale lost nothing by repetition. Needless to say, Christian's lordly demonstration of the sabotage material to the two young workmen likewise demanded a full report; but Leo had no sooner embarked on that than Christian cut in.

'Well, I had to do something to show them we were reliable people and not trigger-happy fools. You were fumbling like a pair of electrician's apprentices, you and Holger. Upon my word I nearly called you over to the demonstration.'

'And we've been thinking you were pleased with us at last,' said Leo, mortified. 'We were just feeling so proud of ourselves. And ot you.'

'There's really nothing at all to brag about,' answered Christian curtly. He got up and started walking up and down the room.

The wet-blanket! Naturally what we had done was no great exploit, but it was our first sabotage, after all, so why should we be so forcibly squashed? Were we boring him now with our foolery? Was he sorry he had invited us? Was he feeling embarrassed? Was there only one person qualified to discuss Christian Borck? Or was he simply on edge, as he had been when I first met him? Gerda didn't put in an appearance, and the sounds from the kitchen had long since ceased. What a time that bit of supper was taking.

A general glumness descended on the room. Jakob and Leo tried to get going again, but it didn't work. They were reduced to sitting in the corner with faint grins on their faces. And

Christian was feverishly pacing the floor. The very man who had shown such coolness and energy half an hour ago now had a spasmodic twitch in his eyelids.

In a moment he would be starting on an idealistic lecture. We should have it explained to us what sabotage really meant. We should hear about the longing to be made use of and to serve, the need to be responsible for something and to give our loyalty to ideas higher than ourselves. About courage and fidelity and a lot more in the same vein. And it might be true enough or it might be a lot of rubbish, but what was the point of saying it now?

We had all stopped talking. Jakob was playing with my pistol, Leo stared down at the carpet, Christian walked up and down. Now he was eating apples as well. I cocked a tense ear at the kitchen. Still not a sound from that quarter, only a disquieting, suspicious lull. Christian might be starting his lecture any time, and the very second he began Gerda would burst into her kitchen-maid's lament and take him in the rear.

It was Leo, of all people, who saved the situation. Recognizing that Christian was now in sober mood, he had the tact to fall in with it by a complete change of subject.

'There's a problem I'd like your opinion about,' he ventured, looking reverently up at Christian. 'Something I've been wanting to ask you for a long time. You're a doctor, so you'll be able to settle it.'

'Yes, well, I can try,' returned Christian, waking up.

'Is it a fact that you can have whooping-cough more than once?'

Christian came to an astonished halt, wondering whether he was having his leg pulled. But Leo's face revealed only an inquiring, confiding deference.

'There's nothing to stop you getting it twice,' said Christian.

Leo nodded gravely. 'No. So I've heard. I know that much. But can you get it three times?'

'I should think that highly improbable. Why do you want to know?'

'Well, it's like this, see,' said Leo, playing his trump card. 'Our mum had the whooping-cough when she was little, and she got it again when me and my brother were kids. Now she's looking after my brother's kid—he's got the whooping-cough, see—and now *she's* gone and started a cough. So if it's a fact that you can get it three times, that'll be what it is.'

One could tell that Christian had not exactly specialized in paediatrics. He had to clear his throat and start again once or twice before his voice slipped into the right professional groove. The detailed medical exposition by which he went on to elucidate, complicate and explain away the case naturally said neither

44

yes or no to Leo's question. It said no more than Leo's common sense could have told him. But here was a field in which he dared not trust to his common sense. It was with all the plain man's superstitious respect for doctors, and all the humility his blunt features were capable of expressing, that he followed Christian's homily. He sat there gaping, more and more doglike and foolish, while the medicine-man filled the air around him with professional terms.

Then suddenly in the kitchen there was a heavy crash, as though a full tray had been dropped, followed by the sound of china and glass smashing. Christian jumped. His discourse dried up, both eyelids vibrated hysterically. He took an uncertain step towards the hall, but I was already past him, shutting the door hard behind me.

Gerda had dropped the tray with the entire celebration supper. The kitchen floor was a mess of sandwiches and scalding tea, bits of glass and smashed cups and plates, all jumbled together.

'Are you going in for sabotage now?' I asked, catching her by the arm just as she was aiming a kick at the shattered teapot.

She turned round with flaming eyes.

'It's your fault!' she exclaimed in a fury. 'I didn't do it on purpose, I was holding on. This damned apron!' And she tore off the symbol of her domesticity and hurled it at the laundry-basket.

'Who said it had to be so classy?' I asked.

'I did!' she snapped, blazing with temper. 'I'd just made up my mind not to be so—not to bait Christian any more.'

'I shouldn't have liked Leo to be drinking tea,' I said gravely. 'I'm sure tea's not good for him.'

'No?' said Gerda. She was breathing hard and controlling herself with an effort.

'No. All he drinks is coffee and beer,' I went on. 'And nothing's happened to the lager, it's on the table in there. So if we hurry and cut a few more sandwiches we'll have all we need.'

'All right,' she said sulkily. 'And I've still got five whole glasses. I think, anyway.'

I squatted down and started collecting the bits and pieces. Gerda squatted by me and lent a hand. Presently, as we crouched there paddling in the tea, her shoulders began to shake. Was she crying or laughing? I gave her a sidelong glance, and at that moment she raised her head and looked up. Then for the first time I heard her laugh. Suddenly her face was alive and animated, and she was laughing with wet teeth in a big red mouth.

She went on being merry all the time we were mopping up and sweeping the floor and getting something to eat, and finally,

45

as we were about to rejoin the party, she dried her eyes and said: 'My poor husband.'

'Sorry,' she said in a low voice to her tortured spouse as we went into the room. 'That was Aunt Kirstine's tea-set. The last five cups.'

'You've managed splendidly,' said the valiant Christian, eyeing me with a certain scepticism, but not unappreciatively.

'Leo!' said Jakob eagerly. 'Mrs Borck hasn't heard anything about tonight's job. Suppose you——'

'Yes, let me hear how clever you've been,' smiled Gerda. 'It did go with a bang.'

'Slick as be damned!' Jakob said, delighted. 'Now let's have the whole story, Leo.'

And in the end it was the liveliest evening yet at Christian and Gerda's.

5

ONE afternoon in April I was over at Leo's garage. It was one of the first genuine spring days, with warmth in the air and a dazzlingly bright sky which made the eyes smart and overwhelmed you with sudden weariness. Working hours were over, and we were sitting alone in the yard in the strip of sun with a couple of bottles and a packet of cigarettes. We were simmering with rage. The idea of starting on our own with the home-made incendiaries had arisen again, and we had seriously considered quitting the group. We felt we had a perfect right to do so. For what had organized work come to? Damn all.

Three days after the sabotage of the speedboats, we had applied the remains of the Copenhagen suitcase-explosives to destroying as much as possible of the big repair-shop on the harbour, which by now was working exclusively for the Germans. There had been nothing amateurish about that action. But that was the finish. We had never been out again, and not a word could we get out of Christian about fresh supplies, let alone regular supplies. We felt cheated and deceived. Jakob had actually talked of going home, he was so disgruntled.

Leo sat simmering silently, red in the face with ill-temper, beer and sun. The vein in his forehead was swelling fiercely, and his whole stocky figure radiated hostility and aggression. It was better not to speak to him when he looked like that, and I kept my mouth shut. I wasn't going to be a lightning conductor.

He really had a surprisingly good profile, with that fair hair, always nicely groomed, that high forehead, the black brows and the perfectly straight nose. But if you saw him full-face there was no chance of mistaking his character or of being misled by regular proportions. Leo had a broad, fleshy face. The thick, twisted lips and especially the swollen eyelids were infallible indications not only of sensuality but of brutality. A touch of refinement in those features and cruelty would have emerged; but Leo had nothing refined about him, he was a rough type sure enough.

Coarse, hot-tempered, vindictive—I could see these words darting through Christian's brain whenever he observed Leo; and Leo had not been slow to confirm this impression by his actions. His hectoring of the workmen when we blew up the speedboats had been uncalled for, to say the least, and his treatment of the sabotage guards last time, down at the repair shop, had led Christian to intervene. With Jakob's help, Leo had overpowered the guards in a twinkling. The poor wretches, who were even more scared of us than we of them, never had a chance. If there was a lack of kid gloves here—well, the disarming had to be done thoroughly. But insult was added to injury. Leo couldn't contain himself. He overwhelmed the guards with jeering and venomous abuse, and he did it sadistically. He took his time. He wasn't going to let them off with knocking them down, he was going to wipe them out. He wouldn't call it a day till he had robbed them of their last bit of self-respect. That was when Christian had stepped in.

All the same I was proud of Leo's friendship, and felt it something of a distinction—not because I saw any virtue in his brutality; not even because of his indisputable good qualities—his fearlessness and determination, his humour; but because he had *accepted* me. For it was impossible to do anything to win his liking. He settled the matter arbitrarily, giving instantaneous judgment on the people he met. Either he took to them, or he couldn't stand them. If he took to them, he was their friend for life; whatever mistakes, follies or crimes they committed, it would make no odds to Leo; he would forgive and defend everything and never lose faith in them. On the other hand, when he didn't take to people, his contempt for them knew no bounds. Even if they were to perform truly heroic deeds to the benefit of all mankind, it would leave Leo cold and only deepen his suspicion. When you asked him what these valuations were based upon, the answers he gave were usually prejudiced and absurd, and yet Leo's verdicts seldom turned out to be far wrong. He had an instinct for people, and like an animal he went blindly by his instinct.

'Well, how about drinking up?' said Leo finally, in a morose voice. He dragged two bottles of lager out of the shade behind the door and pulled the caps off.

At that moment something happened that made him open his eyes, and very considerably improved his temper. A girl came out of the office block over the way and crossed the yard. A little redhead in a black skirt and a black-checked blouse. Her face had a certain resemblance to Leo's. She wiggled provocatively on her high heels across the roughly paved courtyard and disappeared round the corner.

'Who's she?' I asked. 'Does she work in the paper warehouse?'

'You could do with a bit of that, eh?' grinned Leo appreciatively. 'She's not bad, as a matter of fact. Damned if I don't think I'll apply. It can't hurt *you,* after all.'

'Not a bit.'

'No, you've fixed yourself up.'

'What do you mean?'

'Nothing,' said Leo evasively.

The girl reappeared, and wiggled her way to the office door without giving us a glance. Leo followed her movements with his eyes screwed up. And honestly, her backside was every bit as expressive as her face.

'Erna! Hey, Erna!' he called softly. 'What about it, eh, Erna?' When the chit had vanished he added, with satisfaction: 'Low rump, low melting-point'—and threw me a side-long glance, grinning to himself. He put the bottle to his mouth and drank, and said casually: 'So you've taken to cross-country walks.'

'That's the first I've heard of it,' I said.

'Give over, it bloody well was you.' He laughed outright, and looked challengingly at me.

'What's all this about?' I said in amazement. 'I don't get the idea.'

'My mistake, then.' Leo shut up, slightly affronted, on the verge of letting the matter drop. But to be bluffed like that would have been too ignominious. 'I suppose you weren't out for a walk the other day?' he said.

'Me? No-o.'

'Cut it out. I saw you both plain.'

'Both? What do you mean, both?'

'You and madam.'

'What madam? You must have been seeing things!'

'Madam. Christian's wife. Gerda. Wasn't it her you were out for a walk with the other day?'

'But when? And where?' I asked wonderingly. 'Oh, hell, man!' shouted Leo. 'The day it rained! Wednesday! In Ålykkevej. Right on the corner of Ålykkevej and Engvej. I was passing in the boss's old Chevrolet, and I shouted and yelled and honked at you, but nothing doing.'

'Oh, there,' I said carelessly.

'Yes, there!' gibed Leo, scandalized at my dogged refusal to own up. 'How am I to know where else you went parading?'

Actually, I had no need to rummage very long in my memory to retrieve that day.

Gerda in a raincoat and rubber boots, with a red scarf over her dark hair, gleaming with raindrops. Her shining teeth, her blazing cheeks, wet and cold. A black rose in the rain.

The wild light, when it cleared up. The suddenly open sky with blue-black and white clouds. Magic castles with towers and

49

pinnacles journeying to the horizon. And the shadows chasing one another across the meadows.

That moment on the bridge over the brook when she went into a dream and forgot where she was, and slowly woke up and smiled at me.

'If anyone had said you two were a pair, I wouldn't have believed it,' Leo went on. 'But when I saw you walking together——' He raised his voice meaningly and left the sentence unfinished.

'Now look here,' I protested. 'All this because we go for a walk. Anyone would think I'd seduced her.'

Leo shot a glance at me, as though pierced by a sudden doubt: had he got me wrong, was I an idiot after all?

'You! And her! Do you think I've no eyes in my head? Don't tell me there isn't something brewing.' He downed his beer quickly. 'But it's tough on Christian. He's a fine leader. He's got just what I haven't. He can size things up as a whole. But of course he's funny sometimes, and he can't deal with that lass. I see that all right. She's a handful. The sort that's fit to be tied if they don't get the right man. And she can't mope around in that flat everlastingly polishing his silver, if that's his idea. What *does* she do with herself all day, anyway?'

'Nothing special. I don't know. I don't really know her,' I said.

As a matter of fact Gerda seemed to be good at keeping herself occupied. She walked and read, she knew a lot about flowers and birds and that kind of thing.

'The worst of it is that you're pretty well bound to mess things up for us in the group,' said Leo thoughtfully.

'Take it easy. There's no need to make so much of it. It was Christian who suggested her going out with me,' I lied.

But that was stretching it a bit; that was more than Leo would swallow. 'He never did!' he said, staggered. 'Then he must have a bloody screw loose. You don't show the fox into the hen-coop!'

'Anyhow, since when have you been so virtuous?' I inquired.

'I know I'm no angel.'

'Well, hardly,' I said.

'It's not for me to warn anyone off. I know how it is with these things. But the two of you might just watch your step a little.'

He finished his beer, got up and stretched lazily in the final sunbeam.

'Well, luckily there're always girls if there's nothing else doing. And of course he's asked for it. He should have seen to it in time, that we got something to do.'

It was nearly six when we parted. I went to a coffee stall for some supper. After that I wandered about the streets till darkness

50

began to fall. It was a lovely evening, cool and clear. A black-bird, or it might have been a thrush, was singing softly and tunefully from a gable, and one could tell by the sound in the quiet street that spring was very near now. But the trees could still be seen as trees should be seen: bare, with their boughs plain against the sky.

I was rather amused at Leo's anxiety for the group. In general, every weakness of the flesh could rely on his full sympathy—and as for love in particular, he knew it pushed you around as it chose. People couldn't help themselves: and therefore couldn't be held responsible. Leo had formerly praised me for my sound judgment, when I had expounded that point of view.

And good God! I had run into her on the jetty, and we had agreed to go for that walk up the valley—why make such a thing of it? It had come about quite naturally, and nothing whatever had passed between us. I hadn't so much as held her hand.

Still, perhaps Leo *had* some slight cause for anxiety. The walk hadn't been quite as harmless as I made out. Something crossed my mind. Only today, on my way to Leo's, I had met Gerda, or so I thought. My heart gave one thud and stopped. But it was somebody else. Afterwards there was a kind of fire in me. I had had that experience before, but not in quite the same way.

It was the first time I had been to Røndevej without notice. Gerda's cheeks were rather flushed when she opened the door and saw me, but she betrayed no surprise.

'Christian's on duty tonight,' she said. 'He's just gone.'

'Oh,' I said, 'I'd clean forgotten.'

'I thought you would.' She led the way into the kitchen, where she was having supper. 'So I bought that!'

She nodded towards the kitchen table. Between the bread-basket and the side plates stood a half bottle of schnapps. It had been started.

'I don't hold with that,' I said. 'I wouldn't have done that.'

'No, you've always struck me as rather prudish,' she said.

'If one has honourable intentions, one oughtn't to make girls drunk.'

'Gracious,' said Gerda. 'Why not?'

'It isn't fair. They may get hangovers.'

'But if that's what they like?'

'Fancy should be free,' I conceded. 'That's different.'

'And it does you good,' said Gerda.

When she had finished clearing up and putting away, she added, 'We don't want to be in here, surely?'

'We could go for an evening stroll,' I suggested.

We did. We went into the park. But we had walked only a

few steps when the keeper rang his bell to shoo people out. A moment later he caught us up on a bicycle.

'That was the last waltz!' he shouted as he went by. 'We're closing now!'

He pointed out the last open gate, and we strolled obediently in that direction. But we went beyond the gate. On to a bench he had already passed on his round of inspection. Now we had the park to ourselves. We sat down.

What a view! The whole city lay spread beneath us, with the cathedral spire high above all the roofs like an admonitory forefinger. We could see the silos in the harbour, a bit of the outer mole, and a glimpse of the dark woods to the south. Dusk was falling rapidly.

'It's cold here. Give me the bottle,' said Gerda without looking at me.

We hadn't once looked each other in the face this evening. Nor were we sitting too close on the bench. There was a proper distance between us. But now we each had a good swig at the bottle.

'You may think I don't know what you're after!' Gerda burst out. 'But I do!'

'That's fine,' I said. 'Then we can skip the formalities.'

'Certainly not.' Gerda shook her head vigorously. 'It's true I'm a shoddy sort of girl——'

'I know that,' I said.

'Oh. How do you know it, may I ask?'

'I can see it. It shines out of you.'

'As a matter of fact I'm no such thing. I'm a faithful, honest girl, not a beast like you.'

'Beast, indeed,' I said. 'I haven't so much as held your hand.'

'No. But I can easily guess what you're thinking.'

'Without blushing? You should be ashamed of yourself.'

'I can't,' she said. 'I can't blush. I'm a fruit of wantonness, let me tell you. A love-child, got in a maid's room.'

'By a baron and a kitchen-maid,' I wound up.

'A count,' corrected Gerda. 'A count if you please! Don't you know there's rank and rank?'

'You needn't shout about it.'

'Oh yes, I need! You'd better know that I've been found impervious to uplifting conversation, and cross-grained in general with people who want nothing but what's best for me.'

'Poor wretch, then you'll never be happy!'

'I don't expect to be,' said Gerda, seizing the bottle. 'But not for that reason.'

'No, of course you've been unlucky in love.'

'Exactly,' she nodded. 'Do you know this?'

She pursed her mouth and began whistling the wedding march.

52

She whistled like a street-arab. And she jumped up from the bench and began singing the tune, parading stiffly and majestically with the schnapps-bottle in the crook of her arm. Then she whirled about and stood still.

'Marriage is a holy ordinance. It was instituted by God,' she said unctuously. 'I think, at least. In some places anyhow.'

'You're probably right,' I said. 'It would be just like him.'

'Therefore lead us not into temptation, but deliver us from evil.'

She put the bottle to her mouth.

'And I was married at Holmens Kirke,' she went on, sitting down again, 'to Dr Christian Henrik Borck, who's a friend of yours. Please note: who's a friend of yours! He was visibly affected. Why, it even showed in the newspaper photograph next day.'

'You're drinking too much,' I said. 'My turn with the bottle.'

'There were fourteen speeches at the wedding breakfast, it wasn't half grand!' she continued, unmoved.

'And the breakfast was held at the Porta,' I said. That was the only smart place I knew in Copenhagen.

'At the Angleterre, naturally. You're hopeless, man. You could never move in the best circles.'

'What about yourself? I bet you were drunk at the table.'

'So I was. Well, I should think so! On the most beautiful day of a woman's life. But I carried it very well, there wasn't a soul who noticed. Why, they couldn't see straight for tears. They were all so moved at having received me into the family. They were kissing me all over the place. Ugh!'

'What did your father and mother say?' I asked. 'Didn't they come to the wedding?'

'My noble father I've never had the honour to meet. And my mother became a bit of a bitch in her latter days. Actually we couldn't very well include her in the proceedings, but she got a decoration in honour of them.'

'A decoration?'

'Floral of course, nitwit! She's dead, man. D-e-a-d, dead. She's out at Bispebjerg, lying in a corner and observing the by-laws to a nicety. About time, too.'

'What did she die of, then?'

'She had a heart of gold,' Gerda said solemnly. 'You can't live indefinitely with one of those.'

'Bitches don't usually have them,' I objected.

'You're a bit dense, aren't you?' Gerda looked at me with forbearance.

'Yes, very. Give me the bottle. The tragedy of your life makes a strong impression on me.'

'I don't wonder.'

53

'Poor girl, how you've suffered.'

'At first there was really nothing to it. I was given every encouragement, let me tell you. I got grants, because I was so alone and needy and gifted. Just like all the ones who don't get them. But then Christian appeared, and he saw something in me. I was neglected, he said. I just couldn't appreciate all that was good and true in life. Now he would teach me, because I deserved it. In other words he thought I was worthy of a better fate, so in the end he married me.'

'I can quite understand that,' I said. 'What I don't understand is why you married him.'

'Then I'll tell you. I did it because I couldn't resist him. That's all. He was so terribly keen to have me. Why are you laughing? There's nothing to laugh at. It is really very strange to be thought so much of. But what do you know about it!'

'Well, I've never had the experience,' I said.

'Nor had I. So that was one reason. The other was that all that romantic love business my mother believed in when she was young seemed to me stuff and nonsense. It isn't true that there's only one person you can marry. I've known plenty of men, five or six, I could have lived happily with.'

'Then why on earth didn't you take one of them!'

'Now you're being cheap.' Gerda raised her forefinger. 'That's just what I did do. I was very sensible. I looked well ahead and took ample thought, and then I chose the best. Was there anything wrong with that?'

'No,' I replied, 'it's a grand system. Then the right one just turns up. Afterwards, that is. When you're married.'

'I'm a faithful, honest girl!' shouted Gerda. 'Now you know. Cheers!'

'That's a weight off my mind,' I said, 'because Christian's a great friend of mine, and I'd begun to suspect you.'

'Rrrr! How it warms you up! But grrr, it's cold here!'

She moved abruptly away from me. Tilting her head slightly back, she studied me closely. Drunk though she was, her scrutiny was as piercingly sceptical and coldly appraising as when she eyed Christian during one of his discourses.

'What exactly do you want with me?'

'If you don't know that already, Mrs Borck, I really can't tell you.'

'Unfaithfulness is the most boring thing in the world.'

'Perhaps, ma'am, you've been used to a more refined approach and learnt to value compliments?'

'I'm quite equal to a compliment, if it's not too choice,' said Gerda. 'Do pay me one, if you can. But speak plain, because I seem to be getting rather tight after all.'

'Gerda!' I said. 'Lovely Gerda! Never in my life have I met a girl I wanted so much to go to bed with!'

There was a pause before she found the right words. For the first time her quick wit failed her.

'You don't beat about the bush, Holger, I've got to give you that,' she said, and looked at me helplessly. 'But—after that, don't you honestly think the least you can do is—kiss me? Even if I am a—faithful wife?'

It took my breath away. No one had ever responded to me with such total surrender. I had no inkling that it meant so much to her, that she took her passion so seriously. It was almost frightening. This sudden change, this abrupt, dead earnest after all her foolery and pretence, caught me completely off guard. I was swept away in a wild embrace.

When I opened my eyes long afterwards the world had changed; it was never the same again. Not for either of us.

She lay heavily on my arm with her head thrown back, and I looked down at the face beneath me. Gone was the sulky, sarcastic mouth, the aggressive and defiant gaze, all the sullen callousness that hid her true nature. Gone too the irony, the smiles and impishness when she bit her lips, the rapid alternation between desperate gaiety and melancholy. Twice before, her face had looked as it did now: the evening after the first sabotage, and on our walk in the meadows the other day. But not till this moment was her real self revealed. Only in self-surrender, in passion, did she become what she was. Her face had grown, its features filled out, until it reflected purely and candidly her warm, sensual nature—her forehead clear, her mouth full, her eyes dizzily calm and grey.

And there was something burningly sorrowful in those eyes, a bitterness round that mouth as though of need and despair, a sadness and sensual rapture in the whole face, which broke down all resistance within me and robbed me of all self possession.

'Look!' she said.

Following her eyes, I looked up into the tree that stood behind us with its branches projecting over the bench. Through the leafless boughs the sky was dark blue, still wintry and full of bright stars. Shreds of white cloud drifted slowly by, now and then hiding the stars.

'What should we have done without the schnapps?' whispered Gerda.

I shook my head.

'You're not sorry, are you?'

'I'm never sorry. Remorse is a vice, the worst there is.'

'So you do whatever you feel like?'

'Yes.'

'I was so anxious for you to like me. Right from the first time.

55

Things began to matter again, once I'd seen you. But I was so afraid you'd be wanting to save me, and feeling sorry for me, like all the rest of them. That's why I bought the schnapps.'

'Save you? How do you mean?'

'Be unselfish with me, sacrifice yourself to get power over me. Unselfishness in love is a dirty trick. If you always think of the other person before yourself, you're insulting and belittling him. It's perverse. I know, because *I've* been hoaxed into being like that. But I've had enough of it. I'll never, never again try and do anything I don't feel spontaneously. Oh, come!'

I kissed her again, and she gave herself up to me as before.

How did I know it, how did I know those features? For I really did. They touched off a deep-lying memory. It wasn't the usual love-patter, a sudden fancy that she was the one I'd always dreamt of. No, I'd never seen her before, yet all the same her face was completely familiar to me. How? From the glass? No, we weren't at all like each other. The memory wasn't of myself, nor of a brother or sister, for I had none. It wasn't of anybody.

'Oh God!' she sighed. 'How damned hard it is to care when you think you ought. And how easy, when you just want to. Once I was the strongest and frankest creature alive ; now there's not much left in me. Ever since I chose safety with Christian, I've had nothing but conflict in my life.'

'You knew what you were doing,' I said, kissing her hair.

'Yes. That's the worst of it. For it means I deserve what I've got. If you don't follow your inmost, selfish bent in love you land in hell, and that's where I am now.'

'Need you stay there?'

'No. He's treating me. He treats me as though I were a patient in life. All I ever get to hear is what he thinks I can understand.'

'He's afraid of you.'

'No. Forgive me, I'm sorry. It's just that I've never been able to tell anyone, but now I want to talk about it. I know how futile and hackneyed the whole thing is. Come, kiss me, kiss me again. Like before. It's so wonderful in your arms.'

We embraced and kissed again, and said no more about Christian or anything else on earth.

It was as though there had been a craving in me other than lust, a need deeper than I knew of. Something organic, yet mental rather than physical, that she had stirred and brought into being. The effect of these kisses and embraces was the same as though we had slept together. I had rarely felt that kind of satisfaction after merely kissing a girl, and never such peace at heart. In spite of the cold we dozed off on the bench.

How long we slept I don't know, but we woke up chilled to the bone. A thick hoar-frost had filled the lower slopes of the park with a white vapour, which was now creeping up on us.

While we slept, the moon had risen, and hoisted herself over the heights of Mols and peered down into the waters of the bay, had swung herself up over the cranes in the harbour and the rime-blue roofs of the town, up on a level with the slender cathedral spire; now she was skimming across the sky, ice-white and nearly at the full, shivering with cold and her journey through space; heedless of us, she lavished her light on the great silent city, which couldn't understand it, which understood not a mortal thing, which was just asleep.

The bottle wasn't quite empty, but we emptied it now, and scrambled over the railings into the street. I saw Gerda back to Rondevej, and said goodbye to her on the staircase.

That night I slept as though I were lying on the sea, breathing in time with its long, calm swell, and I woke next morning on the beach, with the surf sounding in my ears, the air tingling fresh against my body, and the sun striking sparks from the ocean.

All day I went about in a daze of happiness, with an indescribable sensation of physical well-being. It was heaven just to be in the body and draw breath. And that slight dizziness in the head, which kept making me stop and shut my eyes, reminding me constantly of her.

A couple of nights later, when Christian was on duty again, Gerda slept in my bed.

6

SOON after my affair with Gerda began, Kjeld suddenly got in touch with me. It took me quite by surprise. We had not met since I estranged him by my remarks about Ingerlise, and considering the whole drift of our conversation that day in January, I wasn't going to look him up uninvited; if we were to meet, the initiative must come from him. Quite honestly, our clash had really annoyed me, especially in the first few days after it; but as time went by, Kjeld had slipped gradually from my mind, and in recent weeks I had forgotten all about him.

Why did he want to see me now? Had he some particular motive? Could he and Ingerlise have broken up? Hardly, for in that case I wouldn't be his first choice as confidant. Besides, Ingerlise didn't let go of her prey like that. Nobody who had once got a footing in the yellow villa would willingly be turned out. The chances were, rather, that she had thought the time ripe for allowing Kjeld to meet me just once, so that he could assure himself that I really was what she said and definitely renounce his connection with me.

Even so, I was looking forward to seeing him again, and I vowed not to breathe Ingerlise's name, and so far as possible to avoid all reference, direct or indirect, to their friendship. At least I wouldn't be the one to provoke a final breach between us. With this good intention I cycled off to join him.

It was a fine day. Spring was breaking out everywhere, the world had scents and light colours again. They burst upon you from meadows, gardens and roads at every turn, opening the gate to happy, long-lost memories. That smell of earth and wet grass once caught, the years vanished without trace. The world was in its first dawn, and I was a boy again in a soaking, steaming meadow, on my way to the brook on a summer morning with pail and fishing-net.

Kjeld was waiting for me at the garden gate as he had so often done before, all ready to start. But how he had fallen away since then! He looked overstrained and harrowed—indeed he looked just as though he was practising, in the most literal sense, what he preached, and suffering his way through a youthful conflict instead of acting his way through it. Furthermore, this individual maturing-process seemed to be trying his equanimity rather harder than he had foreseen. The radiantly joyous, expectant air, the light-hearted candour mirroring all the fair prospects on earth, had been replaced with anxiety and irritation. Today, indeed, the enthusiast might have been a puritan.

The change struck me as being so marked that at first I refused to believe in it—so depressing, that I preferred not to see it. You're exaggerating because you're so happy yourself, I reflected. It isn't nearly as bad as it looks. But it soon became obvious that I had not exaggerated. As Kjeld looked, so he sounded. If his expression was gloomy and austere, his frame of mind certainly matched it.

We went for a walk as usual, of course. How we had once tramped those woods round the bay! Hour after hour, for ten or fifteen miles. Along the coast and home again across country. And now on this occasion, when we hadn't met for so long, it was an excellent way of being together, far better than sitting still in a room. We could talk, if we had anything to talk about, and we could be silent without its appearing strange. If the conversation got on to dangerous ground it was easily turned, for there was always something to look at by the way, and never more than on this blue day of spring.

A boisterous wind was up in the rain-fresh, still-dripping woods, sweeping out the last of the winter sourness. Above the snow-white anemones blooming in drifts on every southern slope, the trees creaked blissfully. They were stretching and straining after their long, long sleep, and their yellow buds swelled and shone against the bright blue, smiling sky. In a week or two they would all have burst into leaf, and summer would be here with its green, subaqueous darkness. But what of that? The world was none the less deep and new.

But Kjeld! Here we were, walking through these exuberant woods, and he didn't see them. He talked unceasingly. Nervously, convulsively, angrily, scornfully. And what was his theme in honour of spring's return? The depravity of the age, with special reference to the curse of technology. Yes indeed. This society of ours was soulless and inhuman, the sworn enemy of every creative impulse. Woe to the man who accepted responsibility for it. His doom was sealed. As for the war, what was it but a symptom, one among many, but still the plainest, confirming his theory that the whole of our so-called civilization was a mistake. He actually said that. He condemned it out of hand.

Whereas foreign civilizations, and especially the earliest, which were fundamentally different from our own, had understood what was what. They did so and so.

To which I said nothing. What could I say? The line was so schoolboyish, or at any rate so unrealistic, that it was useless to argue. There might be a lot of charm in this idea that everything ought to be different, but it was the kind of nonsense people grew out of. I couldn't take it seriously. Nor was it like Kjeld to be so sorry for himself. At any other time his vagaries might have exasperated me; today it would have taken more than that to rouse me. I let him prattle on. The wind ran away with half of it, and Kjeld didn't mind my silence. He was doing splendidly without a prompter.

But if I disregarded the text, I found myself listening, though at first reluctantly, to the tone of voice—that queer, broken voice he couldn't control, which stumbled over the words, went husky and faded out so that he had to clear his throat to recover it, and which quivered, trembled and cracked when it had finally become audible. I didn't recognize it. He had never talked like that before. In the end the combination of that voice and the remarkable change in his appearance worried me. There was something the matter with him. It wasn't just ill-humour in general, he was really in difficulties. These outbursts smacked of revenge, of compensation. They were substitutes; but substitutes for what? I thought about it.

Just as I had worked out a suitable preface, the woods ended. We came out on the open grass, which sloped down to the water, and Kjeld was silent. Ahead of us now lay the cliff, our favourite spot and the real starting-point of our walks. We made briskly for it and went right to the edge.

The view was magnificent. Within the bay was the silhouette of the town with its cathedral, grain silos and tall chimneys, for the town grew more and more beautiful the farther you got away from it. Facing us were the heights of Mols, Helgenæs with Ellemandsbjerg, and to the south the Kattegat, Samsø and Thuno, and then the Kattegat again, like a vast ocean, as far as the eye could reach.

Here we had stood in all weathers as on the rim of the globe, and been close to the elements: on summer days, when broad, languid rollers came slowly in over the ribbed sands, making the stones on the beach boil under the surf; in autumn and winter, when huge, solid cloud-formations were moving eastward with shining edges, gilded by the sun behind them, while the off-shore breeze ran light and squally over the bright surface, curling it a cool green and blue. But never had the sea been so turbulent as in today's spring gale. Never before had it been such a marvellous colour, deep blue and almost velvet-soft. All round the horizon the water was in tumult, smoking with white foam-crests, great waves toppling wildly inshore to hurl themselves on the cliff in triumphant thunder.

What exultation and carnival, what a fanfare of springtide and zest for life! You could gaze and gaze over that vast, riotous expanse till you were blinded with light and sun. You could listen and listen to the surf and the gale, letting the noise fill you to stupefaction. You could never have enough, yet you couldn't hold it, couldn't be large enough or thankful enough, before it burst your heart asunder.

Then suddenly Kjeld's voice reached my ear. It rang distinct and quite close, as he said slowly and intensely:

'There you have a true voice!'

Taken aback completely—for at that moment Kjeld and his problems lay fathoms deep—I was on the point of bursting out laughing, for what did one expect to hear just now but a shout of joy? Then I caught the words, and was speechless with embarrassment for him. A voice, a true voice? Of this rollicking, dazzling spring sea? That earnestness was phoney, it was overdone. Life wasn't as damned serious as that.

And this was the man who had found himself! Was it possible to go more disastrously wrong about one's true nature than he had done, and could one ask any further proof of it than that utterance, whether it was a quotation or something he had really thought out for himself?

There he stood, petrified in a tragic attitude. Ostensibly lost, ostensibly unconscious that I was looking at him, but in fact devoid of all spontaneity. I averted my eyes from that poseur, for it wasn't Kjeld. Nor was it Kjeld's eager voice, this ghostly voice that now spoke in the former tone of solemnity.

'Just imagine,' he said—and stopped, so that I might collect and prepare my mind to give due reception to the word of his mouth.

'Just imagine: if the sea were to rise up and engulf that whole tainted city—wouldn't it in all conscience be a merciful death, compared to the one they have in prospect!'

I clenched my teeth, for anger surged up in me which I could hardly contain. But to take this in silence would be a lie.

'Let's go on!' I said, turning my back on him and leading the way. He should have one chance, but only one. And if he didn't seize it . . .

He seemed in no hurry to catch me up. But of course he was musing heavily and despondently as he walked, and therefore couldn't cover the ground at normal speed. In the end I had to stand still and wait for him.

'I'm afraid I don't know enough to do justice to the historical perspectives you've been talking so much about,' I said to him.

'But if the population of a fairly large town hardly matters to speak of, how can you ascribe absolute and incontrovertible value to your own life? Because you do, don't you?'

Kjeld took his time about answering.

'It's true I've no right to, in a sense. But I may have reasons.'

'Well?'

'I'm afraid it would take too long to explain them to you. And strictly speaking I don't owe you any explanation.'

'You owe me absolutely nothing,' I said.

He'd had his chance. Now I let fly.

'I suppose the writing's bogged down just now,' I said.

That was enough. That did it. He dropped his mask on the spot. Exactly as I had known he would. Kjeld was such an innocent he couldn't conceive that I might have guessed his passion ages ago.

'How did you know?' he asked, fiery red and sheepish. 'I'm sure I've never told anyone but——'

'You want to be a poet like the one at the Beach Tavern, own up now,' I said.

'That's right.' He nodded, remembering the source of his inspiration. 'You were there, of course.'

'Couldn't you let me see some of your work? Or read something out to me? I'd be interested.'

'I've done so little as yet,' Kjeld excused himself. 'I haven't really anything finished enough or good enough to show.'

'I'm sure you're just being modest,' I said.

'No, worse luck.' Kjeld shook his head categorically, and I can't say I was surprised to hear it.

'Perhaps it's a naïve question,' I said, 'but how do you know you're a poet? I mean, if you've written nothing that's any good?'

'In a sense I don't know,' replied Kjeld. 'But I feel it, and I don't need any confirmation from the outside world.'

We had re-entered the woods and were walking briskly southward by the path along the coast. The surf was now overshadowed by the tall trees that came right down to the water.

'To be frank,' I said weightily, 'I believe you're wrong. You aren't a poet at all.'

Kjeld took it with surprising coolness, now that he'd been warned. He went so far as to smile. For the first time that day.

'That's only because you know me. A man's neighbours never believe it. Those nearest to one are always the last to believe. Artists aren't people one knows: they're alien, extraordinary beings, isn't that it?'

'Nothing of the sort.'

'Then why? Perhaps you don't think I look like a poet? Real poets very seldom look as you expect.'

'In a way I think you're too like one. Normally you look almost too poetic to be true.'

'Normally?'

'Yes. You've changed a lot since Christmas, you know.'

'And you don't find my new appearance any more convincing than the old one?' There was sarcasm and unmistakable bitterness in his voice.

'You've grown so serious. It seems to me you take things too hard.'

'The unforgivable sin these days!' exclaimed Kjeld. 'He's serious, he takes things seriously—ugh, how unnatural! It attracts embarrassing attention in all good circles.' He gave a scornful laugh and added sarcastically, 'Of course everything that isn't to do with pleasure must naturally excite your deep and particular suspicion. I quite realize that.'

'Maybe,' I replied. 'But all the same I don't believe you're capable of writing anything really important. You're not on that scale.'

'I beg your pardon. I grovel in the dust. Of course you know what you're talking about, don't you? But perhaps you'll just reveal who endowed you with this quite exceptional clairvoyance?'

'I got it from you.'

'From me?'

'From the way you've been going on about the curses and miseries of the age and its hostility to the artist.'

'Do you mean to deny the truth of what I said?' Kjeld was getting indignant with a vengeance.

'I shouldn't dream of it. Only it's not like you to say things like that, they've never mattered to you before. If they do now, it must be because you can't write. You're revenging yourself on the age and blaming it for your own incapacity.'

'Of course that's the only reason you can imagine, pettyminded as you are,' said Kjeld with a snort. 'I've never heard anything like it!'

'What other reason could there be? You should be the last to complain, with the sheltered life you lead, yet you make yourself out insulted and injured. Why? Because you're demanding something that's beyond you. Why else?'

'Spoilt, complaining, moonstruck, pretentious! You've got it all by heart, haven't you? Oh, how well I know it. If anything bears out what I said about the age we live in, it's the suspicion you're casting on me now. Can't you see that yourself?'

'Calm down, man,' I said, 'you're not the Pope yet. It's no disgrace if you can't write poetry, but you can surely stand an objective discussion.'

Kjeld controlled himself with an effort.

63

'I fully realize that I must wait and wait and wait and have endless patience with myself for the next few years,' he said at last.

'You mean you're still too young?'

'I mean first and foremost that I've been late in developing. Genuine talents mature slowly.'

'Then you've ample time. What are you thinking of doing while you wait?'

'No, I have not ample time, as you put it. I have to prepare myself and work on myself. To keep working. Work is my watchword.'

'Technically, you mean.'

'That too. One must know one's instrument, and I've nearly everything to learn.'

'I hope you haven't got me wrong,' I said. 'Of course I'm willing to admit that it may be hard to judge whether a man is an artist, when he's as young as you. And you know one can have a love of literature without being born to create.'

Now I got a little homily. Still, Kjeld wasn't nearly so cross with me as before. If I really meant that, it would alter the case. And quite likely I did mean it, even though my simplicity was all but incredible.

'From a man's background, his parents, his home, his child-hood, his education, his appearance, it's impossible to tell whether he's an artist or not. Those things count for nothing in them-selves. Nor is technical skill, nor even innate talent, the deciding factor. What decides it, what makes an artist, is personal voca-tion. The sense of a call, if you understand that better. The man's own conception of who he is, and what he's to be. It's the call, the vocation, the future, which reacts incessantly on his life, moulding and shaping it and drawing it upwards to its fulfilment. If he has unswerving faith in that vocation——'

'And you have?'

'Yes!' said the steadfast Kjeld—infinitely patient with his in-tolerably slow-witted hearer. 'Vocation has burst into my life. I feel that a poet is what I am meant to be. For the present that feeling is the only certainty I can have, and it's all I ask. There's no more to be said on that subject. As the more mature and independent of us, I should have realized long ago that it doesn't lend itself to discussion.'

'Now I'm beginning to get the idea,' I said, without a trace of irony. 'It's been very nice of you to take all this trouble with me. I won't bother you with any more stupid questions. No doubt you have your own settled plans, on which you're working with a definite aim.'

'Of course I have.'

'I thought so. And naturally you owe me no account of them,

they're no business of mine. I'm not capable either of understanding or of appreciating them.'

'Well, I won't contradict you.' Kjeld smiled with pleasure.

'Oh, I'm sorry,' I said humbly and apprehensively, 'perhaps I've said the wrong thing again, for surely you don't mean to write novels?'

'Did you think I did?'

'No, indeed, and that's why I was wrong to talk about plans. For of course your kind of thing—lyric poetry and so on—is more—how can I put it—well, more extempore, I should say. It has to come of itself, so to speak. More or less automatically. One doesn't actually plan it out. It's the impulse, inspiration that is, that you have to watch for and make the most of.'

We walked on in silence. The waves were clamouring beneath us, and for a time all we heard was the boiling of the surf and the tense, whining note of the wind in the trees. It sang like the rigging of a ship. Kjeld seemed to have relapsed into thought, and kept his eyes on the ground. We were friends again now. Modesty wasn't thrown away on him. It was always encouraging when people knew their place and would own the insufficiency of their lights. It was the first step on the path to self-knowledge.

'I'm sorry if I've annoyed you,' I said anxiously.

'I really don't know why it affected me so strongly, that you should distrust or at any rate misunderstand me,' Kjeld replied, in the strain of fond, feeling self-communion he had been cultivating of late. 'Perhaps I was out of sorts, as you said. Now I feel almost inclined to tell you a little about a plan I've thought of. It might give you slightly more confidence in my powers, and convince you that poetry doesn't come all by itself.'

'You really shouldn't do that,' I said. 'You've no need to justify yourself to me. As long as you believe in your own idea, that's all that matters.'

'Of course you immediately think I'm trying to show off without any justification,' smiled Kjeld.

'That's rather an insulting thing to say,' I rejoined, slightly offended. 'I just don't feel I have any right to know your plans.'

'No, of course you haven't,' Kjeld admitted promptly. 'But as a matter of fact I'd be glad to convince you, of all people—I really don't know why, perhaps because we've known each other so long. I'd rather like to hear your opinion. Perhaps too, I'll understand myself slightly better, if I present my main ideas to you, and get a better view of my own position. But promise you won't let the idea go any farther. I dare say it's childish of me to be so mysterious and so much on guard—but there you are, I can't help it.'

Of course I vowed to keep a still tongue. And presently Kjeld began to talk.

C

It turned out to be a long narrative poem he was contemplating. A mythological poem about the fall of the old Greek gods and the victorious entry of the new, led by Zeus and Apollo. His exposition of the world-order which was then founded in Greece would be wholly personal, and in that sense unhistorical. For he meant to assign to art the supreme influence upon the direction of events. Apollo and the nine muses were not only to establish religion and manage the sacred mysteries, they were also to be responsible for the archetypes of practical life. So if the material was borrowed the originality of his idea made up for it.

Kjeld began very unassumingly, as though he were a trifle ashamed of the project, but soon his bashfulness passed off and he was confessing his grandiose design with child-like pride and self-satisfaction.

He looked exactly like a good dog that has brought its master a stick and expects to be patted as a result. And of course I patted him. I had a heart, after all. I praised his idea to the skies, and he lapped up even my grossest flattery with relish.

'Now I've got going,' he said, 'you might just as well hear all about it.'

And he gave his plan away in detail. I was let into all his technical deliberations; I heard exactly why he had chosen the iambic pentameter, Shakespeare's metre; I learned that his poem would be divided into six cantos of five hundred lines each, or possibly four cantos of a thousand lines each (it would depend on certain details in the course of the action, which wasn't entirely settled yet).

Time and again I warily put in small, intelligent questions. Further inflamed by such a lively interest in the subject, Kjeld threw reticence to the winds. He talked himself warm and enthusiastic, and all his old eagerness came back. Once more his face had that look beloved by all who knew him, of shining candour. It surprised and disturbed me that he could look like that now and there were times when my courage failed me, and I was on the verge of stopping him and renouncing my purpose. Suddenly I thought of Gerda. After all, she was in my consciousness all the time, she was with me everywhere. Wasn't poetry as marvellous a revelation as love? But just when my scruples were most acute, I glanced out over the blue sea of spring rioting in the sunshine, and I remembered: There you hear a true voice! That nerved me for what was to come. I pulled myself together and weathered the crisis. I pumped him systematically, till he had no more to tell; till I could feel positive that every green shoot had been plucked up out of his mind and lay withering in my hand. Only then did I let up, and give him peace to consider just how much he had told me.

'It's funny about the main idea of your work,' I began again. 'In many ways it's so—what shall I call it?—so typical of the age.'

Defenceless and utterly exposed as he was after his long confidence, at that moment he could hardly have borne the gentlest contradiction. And this regular back-hander of mine all but knocked him flat. He pulled up with a jerk, tottering on his legs.

'Typical of the age!' he yelled. 'You call it typical of the age! Are you raving mad, are you out of your wits, man! Is the poet——'

'Let me finish!' I flared up. 'I'm not even thinking of your special—the poet's special—self-chosen martyrdom. What I'm thinking of is that people have grown so damned exceptional altogether. They all want to detach themselves from the majority and be something apart. You can surely admit that! Just look at the way every single one of them tries to dodge the rationing and get hold of extras. No one's content to take his share, they all make it a point of honour to have more than their neighbours.'

'Rationing!' Kjeld's voice shook, he was nearly crying with indignation. 'You're impossible! Clog-philosopher! What has rationing to do with it? Save your tricks and say point-blank that it's the very idea of election and a personal, spiritual vocation you want to crush!'

'I don't want to crush anyone,' I said. 'On the contrary. But I can surely venture to say what I think, without being labelled a snake in the grass. And I think that nowadays the urge to be different is the commonest human tendency.'

'Utter nonsense!' raged Kjeld. 'The truth is the exact opposite, as you know very well. For all those cheap quibblings of yours, it's obvious that you're really defending the average man's vulgar impulse to flatten out everything that's imperishably great and untainted with meanness—the impulse that vents itself primarily on the artist. He's the one they all unite in denigrating and stigmatizing as morbid and unnatural.'

'I'm not talking about the poet—who has the bourgeoisie licking his boots,' I said brusquely. 'I'm talking about the general feeling of being an exception; and I say it breeds resentment, and a feeling of injury.'

'Then you *are* talking about the poet, for you accused *me* of being resentful, and *I'm* a poet.'

'Oh, lord!' I sighed. 'Must you be so personal? Can we really not keep it objective?'

'Objective! Was there ever such hypocrisy! Here I confide in you and tell you about my idea, and you call it typical and banal. You who haven't got an idea in your head!'

'Quite so. But then a purely human ideal strikes me as rarer and more necessary than your poet's dream of being singled out.'

'A purely human ideal!' sneered Kjeld. 'So now that's to be something unusual. What does it mean, anyway? It's nothing but a cliché.'

'If only people weren't so busy standing on their dignity and taking care of themselves! But they'll only accept existence on their own terms. It beats me what they're so scared of!'

'Oh, yes! It beats you,' said Kjeld. 'And it really is very odd! What ever can it be that people are so scared of? Why don't they plunge into the throbbing, teeming, sparkling current of life, and let it clasp them in its strong arms!'

'Of course,' I said, 'there are drubbings and defeats, but what of it? You get up again if you're any good. And don't you always get your deserts? Can anything happen to you that's not in the deepest sense right and fair?'

'If you really mean what you say,' said Kjeld, 'although I refuse to believe it, your ingenuousness is downright shocking.'

'I mean it,' I said. 'In fact it's the only way of living I know. But then I'm not a poet.'

'No. Your motto is simply: Let rip! To anyone who knows you, that's quite understandable. The more converts you can make, the more widespread the general distintegration, the better the outlet for your various propensities.'

'What can one decently assume but that reality is as valid now as it ever was? That it has the same dimensions as it used to?' I said. 'That one can live as simply and significantly today as in the Middle Ages, or whenever, in your view, it was specially good to be alive? It's just that nobody wants to. There's no one left with an appetite for the normal.'

'An appetite for the normal?' repeated Kjeld. In spite of himself, he had suddenly an attentive, listening expression. 'What do you mean by an appetite for the normal?'

'Ask a real poet,' I suggested. 'He'll know. Anyway he won't stickle for his place apart.'

'Of course every poet is linked to his age,' Kjeld conceded provisionally. 'Though as a rule only by his worst qualities.'

'It's in line with something else you once said to me. You said that the poet and the people have experiences in common. The difference between them is that the poet apprehends things while they're going on, he lives the great moments consciously, whereas——'

I was cut short by an exultant shout from Kjeld. He started whooping at the top of his voice, jumping and skipping and dancing a regular war-dance round me.

'The great moments!' he crowed. 'So there we are. You walked straight into the trap! At last I've heard in plain words who it is that has an appetite for the normal and lives by a human ideal. Just as I suspected! So after all you're short of

a fighting poet in the ranks, to interpret your—if I may say so
—costive emotions?'

'If you knew how few we are,' I said, 'the company would
appeal to you. Today it has just that place apart that you value
so highly.'

But Kjeld went on laughing. An exuberant, relieved and
malicious laugh. Now he had me again. Now I was once more
in the toils.

'What was it? Wasn't it objectivity you mentioned just now?'
he chaffed. 'And here you yourself have a little political axe to
grind. I simply won't argue with you. There's not the faintest
chance of equating your experiences with mine.'

'Some time ago I sent you an underground anthology of poems
and short stories,' I said, unperturbed. 'Did you read it?'

'Oh, that!' Kjeld exclaimed scornfully. 'Battle hymns and
propaganda.'

'Naturally, what else. But weren't one or two of the poems
worth reading?'

'And suppose they were, what does that prove?'

'Nothing. Except that there *are* poets who take some interest
in the war.'

'Do you think I didn't know that already? Only it's never the
major poets that you find in such quarters.'

'Not of course the type you belong to. Only those who are lost
in dreams of realization. Like Ewald, whom we read at school.
He wanted to be a soldier and do great deeds, when he was your
age. He never thought of producing art, the idiot.'

Then Kjeld laughed his joyous laugh again. The eyes he
turned on me were dancing with glee, and knew me to my
depths. Yet there was only good humour and sympathy in their
gaze.

'I'm afraid it won't work, Holger! I thoroughly appreciate
your good will, and all your efforts to demonstrate the poetic
utility of the war. Your method was sound enough. Certainly I
only reckon with truths that can take aesthetic form. But all the
same, do you think it would be quite honest of me to join the
resistance movement with the idea of writing about it afterwards? So as to exploit it aesthetically? Because otherwise, I
feel no genuine, personal compulsion to take a hand. Do you
think a true poet would behave like that?'

'Haven't you a propensity to think rather much of yourself?'
I asked. 'We're discussing this in the abstract, and you jump to
the conclusion that I'm out to enlist you. Why, I don't suppose
you'd be any use as a saboteur. It's people of quite a different
kidney we need. My coming to you last winter was an unlucky
mistake. Now I have a far better idea of what's wanted.'

I'm not sure whether he believed this, or whether I struck deep enough to wound him in earnest. At any rate I succeeded in giving him mortal offence. And also in shutting his mouth. We walked on in absolute silence.

Without exchanging a word, we agreed to end our excursion and get back. At the first opportunity we turned away from the coast and made for the open. The sun was already low when we came out among the pale green, springing fields, and the air struck a little colder here, without cover from the woods. The starlings were sitting voiceless in the windy hedges along the road, ruffled and benumbed by the obdurate, day-long gale.

High on the hillside, at a bend of the road, we could see the town again. Behind it, low on the horizon, lay a mass of dark blue cloud, which the sun was turning incandescent and kindling to flame. When the top layers split, it looked as though space itself were expanding and moving farther and farther back. Kjeld gazed intently into it as he walked. More and more fervently he seemed to be drinking in those cold, lucid evening colours.

A stocky little chap, with handsome, regular features, dark brows joined together, and a fresh complexion ; a simple, joyous and positive nature, devoid of contradictions ; a pure heart, burning for all that was noble in life and art ; an enthusiast, whose spine had felt the shiver of an ideal. But an ordinary man, not an artist. A receiver, not a creator. If he believed anything else, it would lead only to warping, overstrain and disaster. Beyond a doubt. Oughtn't I to know him and know what was really good for him, after so many years of friendship?

And he hadn't gone totally deaf to the outside world. Not yet. 'Is it your crowd that have been doing all this railway sabotage?' he asked suddenly. 'Are you in it?'

'We're not cooling our heels. We're well away. At long last.'

After a pause I went on: 'You know the invasion's coming soon. Not in this country of course, but still it's bound to bring in recruits. And the day the English get here we'll have people running to join us from all over the place. On that day there'll only be children and old age pensioners left in the shelters.'

Kjeld, the quick of fancy, looked at me and smiled.

'Then I shan't be all alone down there,' he said. 'Children and old age pensioners. After all, they're not the worst company I can imagine. What do you think?'

7

Far, far above me, somewhere high up in the world, there was a creature that suddenly lost its wits and began calling with its mouth closed. Utterly crazy. As though dumbness itself had conceived and would now have a voice, overpowered by the joy of life, mad drunk with happiness. A demented sound.

Opening my eyes, I looked up into a dense, dark green tree-top, raised on a straight unmoving stem. Too straight. And far, far too high. My head swam, I began falling again and shut my eyes to arrest the fall, so as not to faint.

It was a wood-pigeon I had heard. Then I knew where I was. I was lying in a glade at the edge of the woods. All the flowers of summer grew in the grass around me—marguerites, convolvulus, speedwell, and many whose names I didn't know; but the hedge parsley overtopped them all with its light, white bridal veil, and once too there had been a poppy. A poppy, yes. Red as her bathing-wrap, black as her lap. And as her hair. She, who was lying beside me with eyes closed. Always with eyes closed.

A breath of wind went like a soothing through the tall grass, stirring the broad blades cautiously. They touched one another with a honing sound. Now too I became aware of the sun's warmth on my eyelids and the light out there in the world where the birds sang so shrilly.

But the feeling of emptiness in my head was back as well. As though some part of the brain were missing. Squeezed down into my spine and gone. But now that I was really waking up, at least the leakage had stopped, and my head felt no worse than it had before.

It was my body that felt worse. In my body there was a prostration little short of collapse and verging on—verging on what?

'Self-destruction. Nothing but self-destruction. To be knocked out, that's what you want!'

It was Kjeld's voice, eager and insistent. Kjeld in his room on a winter's day a hundred years ago.

Then was I knocked out now? Yes, I was. I was down for the count. I couldn't get up.

Yet that wasn't what I wanted. No. Something was beginning to work in me, trying to balance things up and make out what was at the back of them. What kind of instinct was it that wouldn't be checked by Kjeld, and was not appeased by sabotage or by Gerda, but still had to press on?

Was there something beyond matter and the flesh after all, something for which they had no answer? Was there something other than being part of life and belonging to it? Shouldn't one, after all, just give oneself up to it? Down at the bottom of it, was there something neither right nor fair? Something that wasn't flesh at all?

What was it I had been in touch with just now?

Suddenly I was falling again. I grabbed out, dug my hands into the grass and held on. A thrill of fear went through me, because I didn't understand anything, and because already it might be too late to understand.

I opened my eyes and turned my head. There she lay on her red bathing-wrap. Naked, brown all over, even across the breasts and down round the hips. But with eyes closed. As always. As I knew. But why, why?

The shadows on the grass and in the wood under the trees were all of a sudden so abysmally black and deep that I felt a burning wish that she should open her eyes and look at me. The dread rose in me again, begging and beseeching her.

Wake up, Gerda, wake up! Wake up and speak to me. Tell me what it is, if you know!

Again the wind stirred the grass, and a shiver contracted her brown skin. I put the bathing-wrap over her, and she curled up in it and reached for my arm. But she didn't speak, and she didn't look at me.

It had been the same all along. At all hours of the day and night she had come and surprised me in my room. On every conceivable pretext she had left home, had deserted Christian to give herself up to me. She was a genius at contriving, and followed ruthlessly where her passion led. And her desire had not grown less vehement with time; it was as wild and consuming now as it had been at the start. But she never looked at me while we were together, and we never talked till long afterwards. Not even at night, when the light was out and we were lying in the dark.

Why not? Was she afraid of seeing above her a face not mine? Or afraid of my face, of finding something alien in it, which would betray that after all I wasn't the man she thought? What was this reservation of hers that I couldn't surmount, what was it she didn't choose to know?

It was dead still and baking hot in the wood. I lay listening to the birds, who knew of nothing to fear, but I didn't dare shut my eyes again. The sunlight was falling squarely on two thick beech-trunks, giving their pale-grey bark a depth and intensity of colour, almost like enamel. Gerda's eyes were like that when they were big and wide open. Just like that.

A sense of desertion crept over me, as I lay there alone. Did we all live only our own private lives, shut off from one another, each blindly obeying his own demon, taking his own course to defeat or victory? Was there no contact between human beings except the short, fleeting one to which they brought only their own thirst?

Leo and Jakob suddenly appeared to me, as they had been late last night, kneeling on the tracks; Leo's face, sweat-streaked and grimy, Jakob with tense, anxious eyes. I heard the noises from the marshalling-yard, where the little engine was rustling and darting about among the goods-trucks like a mouse, giving one of them a jerk, another a nudge that ran through a whole long series, whistling, and puffing off again. Jakob raised his head, startled and attentive, when the first bird woke up and began to sing; and Leo noticed him but just went on connecting the charges.

'It's only a dicky-bird, Jakob,' he said, without glancing round.

And Christian with the stolen porter's cap on. Christian's sharp, but completely expressionless, dead-tired eyes, as he awaited the last explosion. The relief in his face, the sudden slackness, when the explosion came and with it the blasting of every metal on the north-south line, so that all normal rail traffic to and from the city was held up, at least until noon today.

At the memory of that peaceful scene in the dawn a glow suffused me, and I suddenly knew I'd go out with Christian, Leo and Jakob to the magic tracks again and again. Gerda or no Gerda. For some reason I couldn't define. But not to destroy myself. It didn't mean the same after all, what we were doing out there and what Gerda and I were doing here.

All at once Gerda breathed deeply, and sighed with satiety and well-being. She had raised herself, and in one bound she was up, and now sat with her back to me. She shook her hair and screwed up her eyes against the light, then cast a brisk, energetic look around. But the world was seemingly in the same good order as when she had temporarily abandoned it. There was nothing special to claim her notice. She slipped off the bathing-wrap and began studying her toes, which were so well kept—she had been wearing sandals since the beginning of summer—that she didn't find much to criticize, and made short work of them.

Down in the grass there was a small colony of dandelion-clocks looking like day-moons. Gerda picked one of them carefully. Then she whirled round and puffed all the seeds down on my head.

'What's the matter?' she asked. 'What are you thinking about?'

'Nothing. I'm just tired. I couldn't get to sleep when I got home last night.'

'Poor boy, is he so tired?' said Gerda with suspicious tenderness. 'What a shame!' She laughed and bit her lip. 'Christian was worn out this morning too, and yet he hasn't got me.'

'Well, I wouldn't change with him,' I said.

'Do you think you'd be allowed to?'

She picked another dandelion in the grass. This time she blew the seeds up into the air.

'They're like parachute troops, see!' she said, looking after them. 'Just imagine hanging in the air like that, while they shoot at you from below. Ugh, beastly! After all you're well off here.'

She hurriedly flung away the stalk. Then she raised her face to the sun, shut her eyes and sighed again.

'No,' I said. 'I haven't a scrap of faith in any of it.'

'Any of what?' asked Gerda carelessly.

'Of all the motives people can have for joining up.'

'How do you make that out exactly?'

'Well, if I really had we shouldn't be here?'

'Why not?'

'Lying whoring like this, I mean.'

'I'll pardon your use of that expression.'

'Sorry. All I mean is that if one of us, either you or I, believed in anything but ourselves, we'd feel it was forbidden. We can only do it because the personal is what's most important to us and the one thing that really matters.'

'Is there any harm in that?' Gerda asked curtly. 'You sound as though it upset you.'

'No, but isn't it very odd? Nothing on earth can prevent us from doing what we feel like. I feel like sabotaging and so I do it, it's my own look-out; someone else feels like writing poetry, and that's his look-out. Things have no connection with one another.'

'As if that were anything to get upset about. I've never yet heard people complaining because they could do as they liked.'

'Upset? I'm not upset. I don't give a damn. They can bloody well get on with it for all I care.'

Gerda lay down on her belly and peered into the grass. She tore up a grass-blade and held it between her thumbs to blow into it. When she straightened her fingers and pulled, it broke in two. She chose another one, broader than the first, and took pains. This time it worked. She produced a long-drawn yowl, which echoed mournfully and profanely through the green vaults of the woods. She thought this great fun.

'I'm sounding the air-raid warning,' she announced. 'It's like a siren, isn't it? The aircraft will be here presently, just you wait!'

And so they were. Our ears picked up a high, delicate humming, and two small gnats appeared in the air. They took their bearings and made towards us. Then they reduced height in abrupt little dives.

'Mosquito planes! Isn't that what they're actually called?' asked Gerda, smacking one down.

But the two we had seen were only scouts, and a moment later we had the whole swarm on us. Gerda at least was seeing and feeling mosquitoes everywhere, and started rummaging in her bag for cigarettes and matches.

'Boom!' she said, discharging a cloud of smoke at the gnats.

She managed to split the formation and put it temporarily to flight. But the delicate humming sound was back at once. The mosquitoes renewed the attack singly from the most unexpected quarters.

'Do help me, man!' shouted Gerda. 'Ooh! Ouch! Here, take a cigarette.'

'Light me one,' I pleaded. 'I can't sit up.'

She handed me her own cigarette and lit another, and between us we got the midges slaughtered and driven off. Gerda calmed down and stretched herself beside me again. She lay chin in hand, trying to set the parched grass on fire with the live end of her cigarette. The blades wouldn't burn, they always snapped in two suddenly, and again the blue smoke rose vertically. I followed it with my eyes, till it dissolved in air and was gone.

'Tell me,' said Gerda. 'What exactly did we do with ourselves before we met?'

'I don't know. I can't remember so far back. *Is* there anything farther back?'

'And to think it's all owing to the schnapps. Just because I charmed the grocer into giving me a half-bottle of schnapps.'

'Do you really think so?'

'Not really. Kiss me. No, properly. Like last time. Since when have you been taking an interest in what you believe?' she asked presently with her nose in my ear.

'Since that day with Kjeld.'

'What happened then?'

'I told you the day after, but you've got a head like a sieve.'

'Oh yes, now I can remember forgetting because he didn't interest me. It was all so simple.'

'The queer thing is that I was so extraordinarily happy that day. Because of you. I knew precisely how everything ought to be. There was no question of wanting to revenge myself or work

75

something off. But why should *I* mind about his art? Why did I do it, really?'

'For his sake, of course,' said Gerda.

'Yes. And yet I feel I must have had some reason, some kind of ulterior motive for it.'

'Reasons and motives aren't hard to find. But it's not on them one acts in that kind of situation.'

'On what, then?'

'Emotions. And it's the emotions that evolve the reasons. Afterwards. Men don't believe that, but it's true. It goes for them as well.'

'Then that may be what's wrong.'

'It's not wrong at all. It's just like that. And I can't see it would make things any better if you'd had a motive, as you call it. On the contrary. Anyway I don't understand why you're so worried about it all. You weren't forcing him.'

'Ah, that's exactly what I was doing. I didn't just give him advice. I was destroying a chance for him when I made him describe his plan. He can't go on with it now, not after telling someone about it. But I did it on purpose and for the best. I knew what I was up to, though you say it's the emotions that decide, and I was quite convinced of acting for his good.'

'The first time I saw you, you looked capable of trying to smash up the world if you didn't get your way.'

'Be quiet. That's romantic nonsense,' I said.

'Nothing of the sort. It's an answer to what you were asking. I can easily explain why you did that to Kjeld. Because you want to dominate. You think you know best.'

'So I do. I know what's right for Kjeld, better than he does.'

'I dare say. But that's not the nub of it. The nub is that you want to be boss, and are strong enough to impose your will when it suits you. That's what you're like.'

'How do you know?'

'Because of someone who's much the same.'

'Who's that?'

'Have a guess. Just one.'

Now she fixed that sceptical, piercing gaze on me. The same look as she had for Christian when he was intoxicated with talking. Not quite so sarcastic perhaps: there was now anxiety in the depths of it. But all the same I felt as before: that I was being appraised, that my qualities were being appraised; and that I ought to be different with her, truer than I was, though I had no idea how to set about it.

'I hate you to look at me like that.'

'Oh,' said Gerda. She didn't take her eyes from me.

'You're weighing me and finding me too light.'

'No, not too light. Too heavy. You both want power, don't

you? That's what attracts you about sabotage: it means power, now and perhaps later on as well.'

'Nothing of the sort. It's too easy to have power. And I don't need power. They can all do as they please as long as I've got you.'

'Now you're lying, and you know it. You have me, and yet you don't give up sabotage, do you?'

She smoothed the grass at her side with one hand, and discovered a little dandelion where we had been lying. It had been well squashed, but it was in bloom, it was yellow, and it was something of a rarity so late in the season. Gerda picked it, and twirled it in her hand a few times as she studied it.

'Have you ever though how many yellows there are in spring and early summer?' she said. 'It starts with winter aconite and crocus and pilewort and coltsfoot. Then there are the dandelions and buttercups. And let me see, laburnum and broom and bird's-foot trefoil. And forsythia and lupins and roses. And really the grass is yellow in May, isn't it? And the woods, when they're just coming into leaf. And my new skirt's yellow. And even my sandals are a little bit yellow, don't you think?'

She smiled gallantly. Girlish and pathetic. I put my hands behind her head and kissed her eyes.

'All perplexities relating to intellectual warfare must in future be referred through the proper channels to your group leader,' she said. 'That reminds me, do you know what Christian told me the other day?'

'No?'

'That I was so easy to get on with nowadays. Ever since you'd been coming to the flat. He felt that we should see a bit more of each other, and I should go out with you now and then.'

'I'm afraid I couldn't stand seeing you any oftener.'

'No, I've noticed that. You're getting a little tired of me.'

'Yes, very. But if you'll wait a moment——'

'Do I understand that you have arguments capable of refuting me?'

'More or less.'

'We'll just wait a bit, then?'

'By the way, Christian once used another odd expression,' I said later. 'He told me the men we needed——'

'I've no doubt he said *we*. If he'd only be content to speak for himself.'

'He said the men he wanted to get hold of were those for whom personal and general problems coincided. The thing was to convert ideas into instinct, he said. And to embody one's values. At the time I didn't exactly see what he meant.'

'But surely you do now?' Gerda looked gravely at me.

'Not quite.'

'Well then, you must be slow in the uptake, Holger dear, for the pair of us hardly do anything else when we're together but embody our values. Oh, oh!' She rolled over on her back, shouting with laughter. 'Oh dear, what a shame I can't tell him, when at last, for once in a way, I'm doing as he says!'

'Do you really think he has no idea about us?'

Gerda's laughter burst out again.

'You can set your mind at rest. That wasn't why he said it. No, he was just thinking of himself, the sanctimonious prig.'

'I like Christian,' I said.

'A fine fellow he is, to be sure,' laughed Gerda.

The conversation got stuck. It had got stuck before, at this very point. The heat was now rather too much of a good thing, though luckily the wind had begun to stir; at a breath from across the bay, there was a faint soughing of leaves high up in the tree-tops.

I thought of Christian. Long before the sabotage got under way we had learnt to respect Christian's gifts as a leader, and they had emerged still more plainly now that the actions were so frequent: his breadth of view, coolness and firmness, his knack of sharing out the work so that each of us always had just the job he was fitted for. Yet Christian's finest quality, the most admirable thing about him, was entirely personal. It was his self-discipline. He wasn't physically strong. I knew from Gerda what his wretched nervous system cost him in the way of headaches, sleeplessness and neuralgia. Yet not only could he wipe out this handicap and be our leader, but in every crucial situation he was the quickest and toughest of us—the best physically: because he knew himself, kept his weaknesses in mind and met them half way. So will and character counted for a good deal, for more than the body itself.

'Christian's a clever fellow,' I said.

'Is it because he has such a lot to say that you think he's clever?'

'He can ride everything to death, I know that. But after all it's surely some sort of courage that makes him say—and stand by—all the things that normally one can't mention.'

'Courage!' Gerda opened her eyes. 'Christian isn't brave. He's a weak man who talks away his weakness if he's given the chance.'

'Do you really think it detracts from him that he's not brave by nature, when he's able to overcome his fear?'

'Christian doesn't really overcome anything. He only appears to. *I* have to foot the bill, and I know at least one person he's always been dead scared of.'

'It's just that I think he's a much better man than I am.'

'What is it to me that he's good, when he's afraid of me! If you'd said a better person instead of a better man I could at least understand you. Morally, of course he's better. Oh yes, there's nothing he won't do for you, as long as he doesn't have to give himself. There he invariably draws the line. Self-respect isn't exactly his strong point.'

'Well, you stab him in the back if he exposes himself. Really, Gerda, you're too rude to him. Strictly speaking you should distrust me and not him; he's the one you're married to.'

'Oh God. You don't know the first thing about it!' Gerda had sat up, her voice quivering with resentment. 'Why, everything in me was open to him, he had only to let go and accept, but he was too small to accept, he didn't want love, and he still doesn't. Instead he taught me to be ashamed of myself, and for that I'll never forgive him, never! Until I met Christian I wasn't aware that anything I could feel or do might be unnatural. I believed the essence of life was clean and fine. And so it shall be, do you hear? It shall be as I believe! I won't hear of anything else!'

I caught her by the shoulders to quieten her, but she threw me off, drawing the wrap round her. She had clenched her hands, and her eyes were ablaze with anger.

'There's only one thing in the way, and that is that I'm married to Christian. But it needn't bother us more than we choose, so why must you remind me? Forget it! It's none of your business!'

'Gerda, Gerda darling, forgive me! I said that because I'm only capable of action. Sometimes I get frightened because I don't know a thing about myself. Because I'm so damned stupid.'

Suddenly her face was right above me, open and impassioned: that face familiar to me before I had ever seen her, touching a buried memory in me. And all at once I knew what memory. It was of myself after all. Not that she was like me: but if I could climb down to the bottom of myself, as to the bottom of a well, I should find those features there—that round forehead, those thick, dark brows, that vehement, full mouth, those very lines, that soul-pattern—as the sign of my destiny. Now I knew.

'Yes, you're stupid, you're so beautifully stupid, and I love you for it! I've met men who knew everything, who were ten times cleverer and handsomer than you, but it's you who have obsessed and enchanted me, you I think about all day, you who are with me at night when I suddenly wake up—you're the only thing there really is. You've kicked down the wall of defiance and cynicism I had round me, and everything's getting back to what it was before Christian appeared. I'm free and happy, and it's your doing, all your doing, and then you want me to distrust you and my feeling for you. You must never say that again, you make me so frightened, all my confidence is gone, and I can't bear to lose you, I can't live if you're lost to me, do you hear, you mustn't, mustn't ever leave me, forsake me, never, never, never!'

79

Her voice, rapid and low, was already dizzy and stumbling over the words, and in her grey eyes darkness was welling up: the darkness which would engulf the light and reach to the world's end as it settled over me.

'You mustn't shut your eyes now,' I whispered. 'You're to look at me!'

The shrill bird-voices again in the green wood. And among them, somewhere a long way off, the cuckoo beginning to call. Four, five, six, seven, I counted. Then it left off and flew away, and there was a moment's terrified silence among the other birds.

Seven years. Only seven. But not in the war, then. In seven years the war would long be over.

Suddenly the cuckoo was back. Much louder this time. It must be quite close. It was surely sitting on one of the fence-pales at the edge of the wood. And now it was quite uncontrollable. It kept on calling. It laughed and laughed, crowed and triumphed, gloating endlessly over its underground exploit and recklessly promising us eternal life.

I lay with my hand in her black hair. There was a tenderness and a luminous mildness in her features that had never been there before. Something gleamed at the corner of her eye, and a tear, which no one on earth was to have seen, fell on her brown arm and down on to the bathing-wrap. One tear. Only one.

I put my mouth to her forehead and shut my eyes again.

'Hark at the cuckoo, Gerda! We're never going to die.'

She thrust her head down under my cheek and snuggled close.

'You!' she breathed in my ear, keeping her lips there. 'You. I'm happy now!'

8

THE war was going well all over Europe that summer. The Russian offensive was rolling down through the Baltic countries and deep into Poland, and practically every other day brought a communiqué about conquered towns. In Italy the English had reached Rome by the beginning of June, and the day after, on the morning of the 6th, the long-expected landing in Normandy took place. In spite of the furious German resistance, we felt certain of the result from the start. It was only a question of time, of when the front against the invasion forces would finally collapse. And all around in the occupied countries the oppressed peoples began to stir. Denmark's sign of life was the big strike in Copenhagen, which spread to a number of provincial towns, and when the attempt on Hitler's life came in the middle of July it produced all sorts of rumours and anticipations of a sudden end to the war.

In our little local war with the north-south Jutland railway things had likewise fallen into a settled routine. The distributing teams now kept us so regularly supplied with arms and explosives that we were able to start two small dumps in the suburbs. And what was quite as important, the invasion speeded up our intake from the military groups. More and more would-be participants were applying—so many that in the course of the summer four new sabotage groups could be set up. That meant that the town now had six blasting-groups in all, and for the sake of order and method the committee had to apportion their spheres of activity. Christian's group got the southern line, the one that had always enjoyed our most assiduous attention.

The course of the actions themselves remained astonishingly peaceful. We had never yet been surprised, in fact we had met with no difficulties worth mentioning, so that if we wanted to smell powder, as Jakob expressed it, we had to resort to the natural shooting-range he and Leo had unearthed in the woods a good way south of the town.

81

D

But while the course of outward events grew steadily clearer, my own existence was getting more and more beset with problems. Christian and Gerda were on holiday in Zealand, at some fashionable place infested with snobs and lechers. They had gone off just before the strikes began, and I was left to do without Gerda for more than three weeks. It was a consolation that Christian would be away at the same time. Leo, Jakob and I had been secretly counting on his holidays to have the chance of a little private fun, and of finding out what we could do on our own. And then the next thing was an order from the Council of Freedom, suspending sabotage as long as the strikes lasted, and for some time afterwards—so as not to give the Germans too glaring an excuse for reprisals against the population.

So there we were. What a let-down! Jakob went straight home to help on the farm now that it was getting near harvest-time, Leo turned to Erna the redhead and slept with her morning, noon and night, and I had only too much time for reflection. It was a tough job carrying on underground activities in more ways than one as I was doing these days, but this inactivity was worse. I missed Gerda, of course, even more than I should have done otherwise; not for a moment was she wholly out of my mind. In all the girls' faces about me I kept looking for her features, for the slightest trace of her, something in the mouth or around the eyes to suggest her: but no, I never found the least resemblance. There was no one like her in the world. Then all of a sudden her face would smile teasingly at me from the opposite wall when I happened to look out the window. From the wall of my room, from the newspaper I was holding, the pavement I walked on, the road I cycled over, everywhere I went—suddenly she was there and laughing. Twice she came towards me in the street. Fully visible, in broad daylight. It was her very self, her walk, her gestures. There could be no doubt of it. Hot with joy and with a heart that suddenly filled my whole chest, I went up to her—and saw the vision dissolve into the wavy, shimmering summer air above the asphalt. Each time disappointment kindled in me a rage of desire. I must, I must have her for myself, cost what it would. It was the whole point of my life, that I should have her. Apart from that certainty, nothing mattered. The war could look after itself, the group disintegrate, Christian go to hell. She was my girl and mine alone. Didn't everything in her being answer to mine? And ten minutes later I was affirming with a feeling of cold certainty: If I want to have her, I will: for will always triumphs, and life yields in the end.

And yet to think like that was like toying with the thought of a crime. My feelings for Christian oscillated between contempt and shame: contempt because he didn't see through us, like everyone else who saw us together; shame, because I was so basely deceiving him and betraying the trust and confidence he always showed me.

All these wretched lies and deceits we were foisting on him, the whole vulgar, ignoble tissue of concealment! I wanted to get out of it, and then it could still be managed, it wasn't too late. But then I would have to resign Gerda of my own free will, for Christian couldn't take her from me, and that was an impossible thought. My feeling for her refused to be kept down, and got the upper hand every time. Yet it wasn't because I was thinking less about Christian now than I had been. On the contrary. The more I thought about him the less I succeeded in remaining indifferent and the harder it grew to leave him out of account.

I became nervy and lost my appetite. At meals I got stomach-cramps and felt sick, and my heart was hammering and thumping till it could be seen through my shirt. I was conscious of it every hour of the twenty-four, and there were moments when I thought it would stop, but it just went on, it was holding out only too well, and I was awake, awake, insufferably awake and tense, and couldn't relax.

The days came and went. My body was such a burden to me that all I could concentrate on was listening to the wireless. And if a night came when I really did get to sleep, I would wake up with a headache and leaden limbs, as though knocked out by a blow or a couple of weeks of fever. But I hardly ever slept. The nights were a hell of unfulfilled desire, jealousy and remorse. And of heat.

That unendurable heat! There wasn't a breeze in that parched, torrid war summer, or a drop of rain. It was white-hot, pulverizing sunshine from a colourless sky day after day, week after week. Now and then festering clouds gathered in the sky, on rare occasions they might come near enough to obscure the sun for a few minutes, but that was all. It never ended in rain or thunder, only in a weak, distant rumbling below the horizon.

No rain, no friends and no sabotage. No money and no tobacco. But first and last no Gerda.

Only in the twilight, in the hours after sunset, was there a touch of cool in the air. When the children's shrill, everlasting clamour in the street had stopped, and the quiet and dark brought a wind of mildness, loosening the knot in my chest—then at length I could breathe deeply and in peace.

One dusk, as I was sitting in my room with the lamps unlit, there was a ring at the door. I thought it would be Leo, red-eyed and worn out. I was expecting him. He had promised ages ago to scrounge some tobacco for me. But it wasn't Leo. It was Kjeld.

He didn't look over-cheerful, I must say ; nor was I overjoyed by his visit. Nevertheless it was hullo-hullo and fine to see you

83

and how are you and yes thanks and same to you and what a long time it's been.

Kjeld made himself at home in my one comfortable chair: downcast, but not despairing. In contrast to our last meeting, he was himself now—so far as I could see, in the dusk. But he reeked of impending confession. He sat there composed and subdued, watching his chance and without a thing in his head but the desire to unburden himself. The first opening would release a torrent about his trials and tribulations. I resolved that he would wait a good while for his opening.

Our conversation hadn't got beyond the routine stage when it dried up, and I did nothing to revive it. Doggedly I kept my mouth shut, as he did his, and for a long time we faced each other in silence, while night pressed in through the open window, slowly filling the sultry room.

'Surely I can smell cornfields?' he said, sniffing—he was nearest the window. 'Can you really smell them from here?'

'Yes. Why not get into the country for a bit? It'll do you good.'

'It's too late now. Besides, I just don't feel like it. Not any longer.'

'Aren't you going away at all this year?'

'Mother and Father have gone, but I stayed behind on purpose. I wanted to work.'

Silence again. A night-moth at the window, and a far-off tram screeching miserably on a curve.

'Shall we go to the movies?' I said, though the idea of a hot cinema reeking of people was downright nauseating. Still, anything but this.

'Let's not,' said Kjeld, smiling.

'Go for a walk, then?'

'Is there anywhere special to go?'

It had grown quite dark outside. The sky was starless and overcast, and there was a smell of rain. Two heavy, uncertain drops fell on the pane. At last, at last.

Just then a pistol went off in the next street. It sent a loud sharp echo through the whole neighbourhood. I went to the window and peered down.

Three Wehrmacht soldiers, mere boys to look at, came tramping round the corner in their nailed boots. They were laughing loudly and feverishly.

'The Wehrmacht,' I said over my shoulder, 'that's all. They're thoroughly on edge now.'

The shot roused the wind. It started up out of its sleep, rushed through the trees lining the pavement, viciously rattled the open window, and flew up over the roof-ridge and away, looking for some quieter place.

'Something's happened that I want to tell you about,' Kjeld

said behind my back. 'I must talk about it to someone, and I've no one but you. That is if you can be bothered.'

If I could be bothered! As though he were leaving me any chance of escape. As though I ever did anything else but listen to people's confidences, these intimate confessions, for ever more. Why the hell should they all confess to *me*?

'You see I've no one else,' he piped pathetically, and then I knew the whole story! It was about Ingerlise. Soon Kjeld would be admitting that there had been some truth in my view of her after all; yet I had never felt so little satisfaction at the prospect of scoring.

I had meant to pull the blackout curtain and turn on the light. Now I gave up the idea. Sitting in the dark I could at least keep my expression to myself, and besides he would surely get through it quicker if there was no one to look at him.

'In a certain sense you were right after all, that time you warned me against Ingerlise,' he said, preparing to make a start.

Here it came.

It appeared that their relationship had never been much to boast of. Neither had put too much into it, let alone sacrificed anything to it. Kjeld had his personal development and his scribbling to look after, Ingerlise her smart acquaintances in local society, which naturally had to be kept up in case Kjeld wasn't a genius after all. However, they had had no end of wonderful discussions on the nature of love. He couldn't deny that, even now. Nor did I question it.

I could picture the whole scene. Ingerlise, shy and exquisite in Kjeld's armchair, with her legs drawn up and her chin propped gracefully on her hand—the perfect pin-up; and the sacrilegious Kjeld, on his divan three or four yards off, never dreaming of molesting this perfect being who had descended so graciously to his humble abode. They would lend each other a sentimental ear, both just waiting to get in sensitive remarks of their own. All the feelings they would have felt for each other if they had been able, and dared, were brought gingerly out, peered at, described, analysed, and goodness knows what. Exhibitionism pure and simple!

Finally Kjeld had a suspicion that there was something wrong. He was getting to feel so strangely empty inside. Since the day he told me about his long mythological poem, he had been having great difficulties with his work, and Ingerlise hadn't been able to remove them. Then it had suddenly struck him that love—meaning his affair with Ingerlise—might be the snare in which his higher ambitions were trapped; that in certain cases, meaning his own, it might be a distraction, a stop-gap, bluntly speaking a substitute for the real thing, which was and remained creation itself.

On recognizing this doubtful relation between art and passion he had withdrawn slightly from Ingerlise, and what happened? It was the old, old story. What always happens when any little goose notices you can do without her, now happened with Ingerlise. She at once observed the change in his manner, and blew hot as he blew cold. She voluntarily gave up the outings with her rich friends, and even offered to drop them entirely and bind herself unreservedly to him.

That did it. To think that the friendship that had had such infinite meaning for him should be subject to the cat-and-mouse tactics that govern the pettiest relationships between man and woman! That was bitterness indeed. His theory was confirmed, and that was that. He wouldn't let her deflect him a moment longer. For the first time, Ingerlise found herself dropped. It was in early summer that they had broken off, and Kjeld didn't fail to express his astonishment that he had been able to dismiss her from his heart with so little anguish.

So now the way was open for creation. But here Kjeld had had the most painful surprise. For if progress had been mediocre while he was still seeing Ingerlise, it became non-existent when he stopped seeing her altogether. Inexplicably his emotional life had run dry. All summer he had sat in his room gazing into space, without one decent line to show for it.

Then only a week ago a nameless prompting had brought him to the town. Lost in his own sad thoughts, he had wandered down the main street, and in the court photographer's window, who should confront him, with a pensive and soulful gaze, but Ingerlise! The town's Picture Of The Week. Her photograph literally gave him a shock. Warmth and feeling surged up in him, inundating suddenly the helpless dryness of his despair, so that for the first time for months his being was astir and rich. In a peculiar state of mind which was relaxed and intense, painful and pleasurable all at once, he had roamed about the town, till he recognized his defeat: as yet poetry was beyond him. But if he couldn't create, he could at least keep himself open and alive. At the sight of Ingerlise's picture he had rediscovered himself, and he saw that he could only remain true to himself if he acknowledged his feeling for her. She alone could save him. So that after all it made no difference what I, Holger, had said— it wasn't her intrinsic qualities that counted. It was simply the emotion she had the power to rouse in him.

Once all this was clear in his mind he had gone straight to a telephone booth to ring her up, and had no trouble in getting permission to call on her in her room that very evening.

While Ingerlise was making tea, and before they began to talk seriously, he had been sitting fiddling with the wireless. And suddenly, through the welter of ridiculous operettas, jamming

86

stations and stupid propaganda and news bulletins, pierced a violin concerto. Mozart. A real Mozart concerto, so full of youth, innocence and joy, so indescribably pure and flowing and tender. To think that such a thing should still exist in this crazy world! So the true and beautiful was invulnerable and enduring, and he, Kjeld, had no cause for grief. In the slow movement, when the violin began to climb—rising ecstatic, dizzy, yet with a deathless inevitability towards perfect bliss—he forgot everything around him, even himself. But just as the music was going to escape from earth altogether and be one with the divine, the siren on the roof opposite broke in with an alert.

He had felt so shattered by this collision between two essentially different worlds that he thought his heart would break. So crushing was this defeat of all he loved and believed in that he burst into tears. If not even Mozart could be safe from destruction, what was the point of anything!

'Ingerlise was awfully kind and sympathetic,' said Kjeld. 'We didn't go down to the cellar, we stayed where we were, though they were shooting over the house the whole time. But I suddenly didn't give a damn. I don't know what came over me. I let go altogether. And then—well, it ended as I suppose it always does when you're with a girl.'

'At last,' I said. 'Congratulations! For I take it she didn't actually have a hole in her back like the elf-girls.'

Kjeld said nothing. But through the dark he reddened like a tomato.

'Good Lord, Kjeld, it was the first time for both of you, and it needn't be any less genuine because it's a failure. Next time you——'

'There won't be a next time,' Kjeld said tonelessly. 'The day after, she wrote and said she'd rather not see me again.'

'What? Why not?'

'I don't know. She wrote that in future she must seek out more mature company.'

'She *what*?'

'She wrote that she must seek out more mature company. I was nothing but an overgrown puppy. That's how it went.'

It was really too despicable. And just when I'd thought him safe and over the worst. The bitchy little snob! At that moment I could have killed her.

'You didn't deserve that,' I said. 'You're much too good for that sort of treatment. And it's too bad if you were expecting her to act decently, for of course she's always got to tart things up. All the same this is a bit worse than I'd have expected, I must admit.'

'It wouldn't matter so much,' said Kjeld, 'that her—well, that she wasn't equal to—and that she was so—I don't know what

87

—so unnatural. The worst of it is that I've forgotten all my ambitions. I can't even recall what used to be the point of my life. The whole thing's become unreal to me.'

'The point will come back all right, next time you're inspired,' I said reassuringly. 'As long as you don't give up altogether. But of course it takes a day or two to get over a filthy trick like that.'

'It's doubtful whether I really have those gifts,' said Kjeld slowly. 'I don't think so now. I suppose it was a delusion after all.'

'Surely not. It's just that you're too impatient. Why should you be one of the boy-geniuses? Give yourself a year or two.'

'The state of emergency is cancelled,' replied Kjeld, and I could hear the sad little smile in his voice. 'I'm on the same footing in life as anyone else, so now there's only one decent course for me. Isn't there?'

I got up, drew the blackout curtain and turned on the light. He didn't look much the worse for wear. Certainly his fine eyes were wistful, and his whole countenance was rather downcast; but it had the stamp of resolution. The mouth was firm and decided. Once before, I had seen him with that oddly determined look.

'Shall we get a breath of fresh air?' I asked. 'I have to go out for a moment.'

'I'm ready any time,' said Kjeld. He was on his feet at once.

'It's only a message I have to give before ten o'clock,' I explained as we were going downstairs.

Kjeld's smile said he knew better and had caught on.

It had rained just enough for the pavement to be wet, but in spite of that warm, gentle summer rain there was something ominous and sinister in the air. The southern sky was now flashing fiercely and thunder rolled with hardly a break; but the storm was several miles away, and *that* wasn't where the threat came from. No. Some Thing was lurking round the next corner, ready to spring at your throat. The streets were so empty and forbidding that you would have thought it was curfew-time, or an alert with bombers overhead. Everywhere that lurking, tense silence, all ready to snap.

We hurried on and didn't meet a soul on the way.

At the mouth of an alley in the old town there was an old-fashioned street-lamp on the wall, the kind a watchman used to light with a torch. Here I asked Kjeld to wait a moment. He seemed quite nonplussed when I left him, and the resolute, initiated look on his face suddenly gave place to one of doubt and loss of assurance.

I was away ten or fifteen minutes. Longer than was necessary, but I took my time on purpose.

On my return, Kjeld was leaning against the wall with his back to the alley. The raindrops glimmered in the subdued yellow lamplight as I came up to him, and I gave him a cheery thump on the back to indicate that I could now be on my way. Kjeld didn't take the hint. He just stood there, and I had to stop and wait for him.

'Sorry it took so long,' I said. 'There's nothing wrong, is there?'

He made no reply. Made no move. I caught him by the shoulder to turn him round, and saw that he was crying.

'Here, what's up? Are you ill? Did anything happen while I was away?'

Still he didn't speak, and wouldn't look at me. He jerked his head, threw me off, and cried defiantly into his coat-sleeve. Like a boy.

So I stood there patting him a bit and muttering such consolation as I could think of. If only he'd stop it. I couldn't understand how he could give way like that.

I was going to put my hand on his shoulder again, but I snatched it back as though he had been red-hot when he flung round and shouted wildly:

'I believed you meant to—how can you pretend not to understand, when you said yourself——'

'Shut up and pull yourself together, man! You shall join all right.'

He'd thought, of course, I was going to initiate him forthwith, this very evening, into underground work; that I'd take him along to the group, which was now in a back room a hundred yards off, planning a bit of factory sabotage. Together we were to have crept into the alley. I was to have groped over the wall for the secret knob, which when lightly pressed would cause the hidden door to spring open and reveal the pitch-black shaft at our feet. With my candle held aloft and Kjeld at my heels, I was to have descended the precipitous winding stair to the gloomy vault where the rest of the conspirators were already gathered. At the sound of our approach, they would turn their firm, noble faces as though numbering off, and demand and receive the pass-word. And in this select company Kjeld would take the oath. Kneeling on the stone floor in token of his admission to the brotherhood he would receive the accolade from the head of the order.

Now that Kjeld had finally accepted the idea, he was sure to be picturing it in some such cloak-and-dagger, romantic form. And of course I understood his disappointment only too well. He had been quite entitled to think I was going to help him. All evening he had been moving deliberately towards this very point. I hadn't been able to head him off it, and I hadn't stopped him.

The mute appeal in his eyes when he first came; his reply that he didn't any longer feel like going away, it was too late; his determination on the way here; his bewildered expression when I left him—it all pointed the same way, and of course I had noticed and had turned a blind eye; I had taken the chance I thought existed, and kept on hoping to evade the inevitable. Even when I found him crying under the lamp I had tried to dodge the issue.

The rain was heavier now, it had started gurgling through the drains in the gutter, and the asphalt was shining. And the thunder had drawn nearer. Soon it would be right over the town. It was no longer continuous, a dull, far-off rolling; you could distinguish the separate claps, and they made plenty of noise.

We couldn't just stand there getting soaked, and Kjeld was quieter and crying less stormily now that he could see I had given way. He came willingly when I linked my arm through his and marched him off.

On our way back to my room at the double I felt wildly irritated with him. It was the limit, to give way like this. After all his sermons on not squandering one's life, on keeping oneself inviolable, he was now revealing himself as a bankrupt poet, fancying the 'cause' could save him! It was ludicrous and outrageous.

And of course it had to happen just now, when my own outlook was so confused. He had to select just this time, when I was in the very worst mood for being a nursemaid, to unload his life on me.

'I can get you into some group all right,' I said irritably, when we were back in the house. 'But hadn't you better think again? For you'll get no more out of it than you put into it, and if you're merely bent on courting destruction, why not a straightforward jump into the harbour? Anyway you can't expect the rest of the group to feel impelled to run any unnecessary risks for your sake.'

Kjeld was out of breath and red in the face from hurrying through the sultry rain, and his colour didn't subside now. My speech mortified him deeply. He asked sarcastically and with an aggrieved set of the mouth:

'Since when have you been so chary of other people's lives? As to whether my motives can compare with yours, that's for you to judge. I got them from you, unless I'm very much mistaken. And this is something you owe me anyway. I'm not having any stipulations from you.'

It was a reversion to our boyhood. I recognized the situation. Whenever the big boys of the neighbourhood set on Kjeld and gave him a licking, because he couldn't resist shouting after them, he came and demanded that I should avenge him, and demanded it categorically, with tears in his eyes at the disgrace he had suffered. If I didn't agree on the spot, he would stamp with rage and scream, 'You owe me that much!' And unreasonable as the demand might be, I always ended by giving in to it. I would seek out one of the big boys, who had never done anything to me, and consequently get the drubbing I deserved.

Now it was exactly the same. It only wanted the stamping on the floor.

'What are you laughing at?' shouted Kjeld furiously.

'I'm not laughing. I'm smiling because your head's so wet. You look like a poodle.'

At that moment the window rattled from the first full-scale thunder-clap.

As soon as Christian got back from his holiday I sought him out and told him about Kjeld. In January, six months ago, we had jointly weighed his qualifications in the balance and found they would do: but Christian had also heard how he had reacted to my visit. My problem was how to bring Kjeld's attitude at that time into reasonable harmony with his expressed wish at the moment. I put my cards on the table. One shouldn't tell lies when it isn't strictly necessary.

Christian was standing by the window as usual, eating apples for the good of his health and looking absently across the bay. I wound up by repeating that of course I didn't imagine Kjeld could join our own group.

Christian turned round and gave me a long, searching and significant look, which I couldn't fathom.

'I suppose you won't actually make a row if he does join us?'

He didn't wait for an answer. He declared for Kjeld immediately, and with such warmth and vigour that it gave me a start. Evidently nothing could be more welcome to him than this very request. It was just the news he had been waiting for for years, or so it sounded. Within five minutes Kjeld was a member of Christian's own group.

Gerda gave me the explanation next day, when we met rather less formally. Christian had decided to leave the group. As soon as he had found a new man and got him broken in, he was going to appoint me his successor and retire.

But why should he choose to pull out now?

Of course they wanted him on the local committee: there was every reason why he should be relieved of the heavy work and given a key position in the organization, and I had long feared it would come to that. But so far as Gerda knew, his contacts with the committee hadn't been specially close in the three weeks they had been away, so it couldn't be 'promotion' that had decided him.

Then it must be the wish to part Gerda and me. He had finally come to suspect—but how? Gerda suggested that she might have said something in her sleep, which Christian, being such a bad sleeper, had overheard. I remembered the steady, searching look he had given me the day before, and I became certain we had really been found out.

In these circumstances it was obvious that Christian would like Kjeld when they met. It was a foregone conclusion; so timely an arrival could not fail to win the utmost sympathy. But there were other, quite solid grounds for Christian's taking such a liking to Kjeld. His attitude to Jakob and Leo had always been uncertain, and it was hard to make out how much he really thought of them. One minute he would romanticize them, the next he would be slightly disdainful—it all depended on his mood; but before he went on holiday I had the distinct impression that he was getting tired of us. Whereas Kjeld, who now came into the picture, was civilized, and it was possible to make contact with him, and—there were no two ways about it—Christian must have felt it something of a relief to have someone in the group with whom consecutive conversation was possible.

Kjeld for his part was astonished, to put it mildly, that a man of Christian's quality should turn up as a group leader in the resistance movement, and the two of them hit it off at once. When they really got talking, as they quite often did, Kjeld would recover his spirits and laugh his old, infectious laugh again.

Gerda, on the other hand, took not the slightest interest in Kjeld. He was too soft and too pretty. No harm in him, certainly, but not good for much. Off with his head!

Nor had Jakob any strong views. If he had had to make a pronouncement—for which there was luckily no need—he would if anything have been favourable, because Kjeld was taking his, Jakob's, place as the 'baby' of the group.

But to Leo, with his instinctive hatred of weakness and sensitivity, Kjeld was anything but welcome.

'Him!' he said scornfully. 'Only a mother could love *him*! And things were just going first-rate. Why did you have to bring him in?'

Christian had naturally foreseen this reaction, and to maintain the inner unity of the group he put Leo in special charge of Kjeld's training as a saboteur. But if he fancied this pedagogic role would bind Leo to Kjeld and take the edge off his dislike, he was sadly mistaken. Leo indulged himself in a dire revenge. He treated Kjeld like the rawest of recruits. He resorted to all the immemorial methods employed by the army, as by every other authoritarian regime, to keep its subjects in fear and trembling. His approach was incredibly harsh. At one moment he was bullying and ordering him about and watching his every movement as though Kjeld were incapable of doing the simplest thing on his own. Then he would ignore him entirely in the most insulting way, and take it as a matter of course that he knew

92

all about explosives and the technique of sabotage. He made a practice of giving him conflicting orders, so that Kjeld would be bound to do something wrong and furnish an excuse for bawling him out. Of course this army discipline was contrary to the spirit in which we usually worked, and Christian did what he could in a quiet way to make up for Leo's bullying methods, though without interfering in the instruction. It was clear that he had determined to stick to Kjeld at all costs.

And Kjeld could take it. He saw through Leo immediately but never answered him back. With a closed, completely expressionless face, he put up with everything, invariably docile and long-suffering. And when you knew how awkward he could be in practical matters, how spoilt he was at home, and how elaborately as the time went by he had planned out even the minutiae of his daily life because practically everything had associations for him, you couldn't help marvelling at his grasp of things. Nor did he appear to be jumpy when we first took him out with us. Indeed he shooed away a couple of rather indiscreet spectators with the utmost coolness and on his own initiative. He was taking pains, and he was doing himself credit. But Leo wouldn't be satisfied.

Leo's 'mother-in-law'—Erna's mother—had a roomy little villa with a basement, which was one of our dumps; and one evening, Leo, Jakob and I were down there unpacking. We had just received part of a new distribution, and this time, what with counting, cleaning and assembling the weapons, there was plenty to do. Leo and Jakob loved this job; and it didn't diminish their joy, that Christian couldn't be bothered with it—on the contrary, is simply meant there was all the more for them.

Leo started on his favourite subject.

'We were better on our own,' he said. 'Nowadays we're getting under each other's feet, anyone can see that. Five on the job's definitely one too many.'

There was no response from Jakob or me, and Leo went on: 'This Handsome's a pretty cagey sort, isn't he? Is he always like this, Holger? Queer, too, because I don't suppose anyone's doing anything to him?'

'Well, perhaps you're rather rough on him now and then,' I said pacifically.

'*Me?*' cried Leo in astonishment. 'Me rough on him? Am I doing anything to him now? I've put him on guard. That's all.'

Jakob showed his long teeth in a grin. He would soon be cross-eyed with squinting down the barrels of all the brand-new Winchester rifles.

'The only thing is,' said Jakob, 'that we've never had anyone on guard here before when we were unpacking. You didn't think it was necessary. Not till Kjeld joined.'

'Do you want him down here?' Leo demanded. 'Is he to be allowed to play with Daddy's tools?' Leo fondly patted the stock of one of the rifles, which was lying on the sack in front of him. 'But that's not exactly what I meant. I meant that I'd like to know what Handsome thinks about. There's always something in his pretty head that shouldn't be; something extra. Perhaps it's because he's a student,' he hazarded philosophically.

'Steady on!' Jakob protested. 'Holger and I are students.'

'I know. But you two don't count. You're sort of exceptions, and of course you're all right. But Handsome'll be playing us a trick one of these days, you mark my words. Sometimes I almost wonder if he isn't an informer.'

We laughed, and Leo himself was hardly serious. But he wouldn't drop the subject.

'Anyway there's one thing I don't get, and that's why he had to join *us*. They're forming groups all over the town now, and they all want men. Why do *we* have to have him? You tell me that, Holger. He's your friend, and you brought him along.'

'Ask Christian,' I said. 'He must have some reason for it. I didn't ask to have Kjeld in our group.'

'Then can't you arrange for us to get rid of him?' He said it aggressively, fixing me with his eye.

'Perhaps. If you can wait a month or so. But in the meantime, suppose we get him so well trained that he'll be an acquisition to any other group. The better he is, the easier we'll find takers, isn't that so?'

'Jakob!' said Leo. 'Go up to Erna's and get three bottles of lager. They're in the kitchen cupboard. And tell her I won't be up just now. She can get off to the cash-desk.'

'*Four* lagers, Leo,' I begged. 'Four!'

'Three lagers, Jakob,' he insisted. 'And a soda-water for Handsome on the stairs.'

9

CHRISTIAN soon realized that the group was less harmonious than it had been, and to reunite us and get Kjeld accepted by Leo and Jakob, thus securing his own retreat, he arranged a week-end near Silkeborg for the whole party.

He had got the loan of a hut in the woods there. I don't know who owned it originally, but according to Christian it had always been at the service of the resistance movement. Two English airmen had been in hiding there at the beginning of the summer, and it was used on occasion by other underground characters when they wanted to lie low. Christian had been there once himself, apparently to a meeting of various brass-hats of the Jutland movement.

We were going by train, of course. The southern railway being our own line, we were in a position to know when it was functioning, and on a hot Saturday afternoon at the end of August we met punctually outside the station—Christian, Gerda, Kjeld and I. Leo and Jakob were late. Leo, who had a sympathetic dealer, was to provide drinks, and we assumed that Jakob was with him—those two had been getting on famously of late ; and so it turned out.

It was Jakob who announced their arrival. Five minutes before the train was due there was a piercing whistle from the main street, and Master Jakob came strutting across the square with his most cheerful grin.

'But where's his luggage, and where's Leo?' asked Gerda, glancing at the clock.

In a moment Leo appeared, pounding away hammer and tongs at the low-geared delivery tricycle—'POVL JENSEN, TROJBORG, GROCER.' He had spread the old grey tarpaulin over the carrier, and looked every bit as standoffish and unapproachable as when he was transporting material to the dumps on the same conveyance. He swept dashingly from the traffic roundabout and drew up at the edge of the pavement, where Jakob stood ready.

'Here we are with the goods, chief!' cried Jakob. 'A little marzipan loaf, lady? We have them pound and half-pound, market prices. Guaranteed fresh, straight from the wholesaler!'

Christian glanced round discreetly, and Gerda laughed. We got the two fiendishly heavy suitcases off the carrier, and parked the vehicle in the cycle-shed. The German sentries were as usual straddling their legs in the station entrance, and Leo and Jakob took extraordinary pains to attract their attention. They handled their suitcases as though they were high explosives, fumbled and fooled about with them, gesticulated and winked at each other, and looked exaggeratedly shady and mysterious. It was exactly like a conspiracy scene on the silent films.

'Bomben und Granaten!' said Leo for good measure, as he was passing the guards. 'Passen Sie auf, gentlemen!'

It would have been all the same if they had been bombs. The two Germans didn't raise an eyebrow. Not an idea went through their heads. They had their orders, and their orders said nothing about young men with heavy suitcases at four in the afternoon.

'Hey, Jakob!' said Leo. 'How about prodding them? I think they're tin.'

'Get a move on, blast you! shouted Christian from the hall. 'Or we shan't catch the train!'

But of course we did catch it. We even got a whole carriage to ourselves.

'Look here, Leo,' said Christian, when the suitcases were finally settled on the rack and all was quiet, 'just how much have you got in those cases?'

'Well, the two of us have saved up a bit,' replied Leo. 'And drawn a bit in advance. So we've got forty-seven lagers all told.'

'It's like those sums we had at school,' put in Jakob. 'If one man drinks four lagers in an hour, how long will it take five men to drink forty-seven lagers? I've worked it out, too. It'll take exactly two hours and a quarter. With two lagers over, I grant you, but *they* won't stretch very far.'

'We were a bit scared it wouldn't be enough for five grown men and a healthy girl,' Leo confessed, 'and so Jakob got hold of a half-bottle of schnapps. That's in addition to the whole one we started with. You know, chief, you've always said we weren't to run any needless risk, so we hope for once you're really pleased with us.'

'I'm very pleased with you,' declared Christian. He seemed disposed to be one with us today, and indeed he had no choice. 'I'm just a trifle worried about how much you have left.'

'We've only had two each!' protested Jakob.

'And if you think that's too much after all our fag with the suitcases——' said Leo.

Christian took the hint, and we had a lager each as the train

96

was rolling under the bridges, past all the dear old spots, the block-stations and points.

' "In these days, so momentous for our country," ' said Jakob, removing the caps, ' "the population must remain united and obey the King's call of April 9th for peace and order." '

' "Let no one take the law into his own hands or yield to incitement!" ' added Leo with raised voice.

' "These chauvinists, these provocateurs of mixed origin, irresponsibly and covertly at work to discredit co-operation," ' I went on.

' "And sow dissension among the Danish people!" ' chimed in Jakob, righteously incensed.

'Scum of the nation!' concluded Leo. 'How can they!'

We looked mournfully at each other, and then wailed in chorus:

'It's hard luck on the old King!'

'You know your stuff,' said Christian. 'The King!'

'O.K.,' said Leo, 'here's to him.'

And we drank.

'Out with the cards, Jakob!' Leo commanded at this point, and Jakob lost no time in complying.

'There's no need for me to play,' said Gerda.

'Nor me,' Kjeld added quickly.

'Of course you'll play,' Leo ruled.

And while Jakob dealt, Leo spun out the pleasure of instructing Gerda in the simple rules, and I watched her mouth and listened to my heart.

Jakob, in the corner seat next to Gerda, was sceptically contemplating his hand. To him cards were a serious matter. He had had a haircut in honour of the day, and the barber had brutally reduced the long, ragged locks in front to a small, floppy forelock.

'You look like Hitler,' I told him.

'Chaplain Adolf!' grinned Leo. It had lately dawned on him in all its incongruity that Jakob was a divinity student, and now he never let slip a chance of alluding to his calling. 'What's Parson's text for today?' he asked. 'Or hasn't the reverend gentleman finished his studies?'

We made Jakob the centre of the party, which put him in exuberant spirits. He basked in the unwonted attention he was receiving, and won nearly every game.

Half an hour later we were getting out at a country halt on the Skanderborg-Silkeborg line. From the shady strip of asphalt we watched the train jogging off again down the single track. When it had gone, for a moment all was quite still and empty. Then the warm, dry summer wind soughed languidly in the trees of the station-master's little garden.

'The war's never reached this place!' Kjeld burst out.

'Is that so!' Leo snubbed him. 'Well, it has now.'

'If you bend down and look through the trees, you can see where we're going,' said Christian, pointing out the direction. 'The house is on that hill over there.'

We looked out into the sunshine over bare, rolling fields. The corn was already in, and flocks of busy sparrows were regaling themselves in the stubble. At the forest's edge, two or three miles off, was a densely wooded hill.

'God help us!' said Jakob, looking disconsolately at the luggage. 'How are we to get all the beer over there? We ought to have brought the delivery cycle.'

But Christian found a way. Though it was Saturday and long after closing time, he went to the village shop, and after a certain amount of parleying succeeded in borrowing a bicycle. With one suitcase on the handle-bars and one on the carrier, we were able to get going.

The village itself was only a handful of builders' cottages and soon came to an end. The last house was a white dairy. Inside it someone was sluicing down the tiles and rattling empty buckets. Otherwise we heard no human sound. Along the dusty lane, the telephone poles were humming, and the swallows gathering for flight. Flocks of them were perched in the trees, twittering their farewell. In the ditch there was still a solitary little cornflower. It was the same colour as Gerda's blouse.

The hill had the wildness of a jungle. Spruce and fir, ancient elders and small white birches grew there pell-mell. A dead tree, suffocated in the crush, lay as it had fallen, across the sandy way leading up to the house. Among the scrub at the top we found wild roses and dark, shining blackberries, and ripe rowan-berries not too high to be within easy reach. Everywhere spiders had spun their webs, and a deep, deep stillness reigned. In the glade behind the house, gadflies and dragonflies stood still in the drowsy sunlight ; and when a tipsy bumble-bee came lurching across the lawn its hum only gave expression to the glowing silence of the late-summer day.

Christian wiped the sweat from his forehead and shed his rucksack on the lawn, where the grass grew tall in thick cushions of moss.

'It may look a bit untidy here,' he apologized, 'but the house itself is fresh-painted. Come and see if you recognize the colours.'

The house was red with blue doors and white windows—the colours of the Royal Air Force. It was the airmen who had begun the painting, and of course Leo and Jakob were thrilled that here two dyed-in-the-wool allies had been plying the brush.

Kjeld was especially thrilled with the view. The house stood right on the edge of the hill-top, facing Lake Mos. The scrub, less dense on this side, fell steeply to a scrap of meadow, and beyond the lake the country slanted upwards in a tremendous ridge. A long, straight line of trees on the horizon indicated the main road running south-west across Jutland.

Indoors there was plenty of space—kitchen, sitting-room, and two bedrooms with bunks—and a sickening heat in every room. We flung windows and doors open for a draught, and while the others were unpacking and sorting things out, I chopped some kindling in the scrub for Gerda's kitchen range.

The evening was warm, and we decided to have supper out of doors. Gerda threw a coloured cloth over the old garden table in front of the house on the lakeside, and we lugged the basket-chairs from the sitting-room to put round it.

There were certainly no deficiences in the meal when it was ready. Each of us must have ransacked the larder at home, the spread was so abundant. Leo and Jakob went straight for the beer and schnapps and made sure there should be no heeltaps. They obviously intended to drink us all under the table. And indeed we were soon getting merry. But whenever there was a moment's lull in the talk, a vast, unfathomable stillness crept up on us from land and sea.

'Peace bloody well reigns in town and country now, eh Reverend!' said Leo, more than half-seas over.

'No, this won't do,' Jakob replied in alarm, 'we must have another. Here, say something, sing something, all of you!' he yelled suddenly, his voice ringing over the burnished water. 'This one! Come along!'

And he struck up a patriotic song. We applauded him and clinked with him and, certain of having made a hit he went right on to Montgomery and his Eighth Army, Tipperary, the song of the Soviet Air Force and The Internationale. He got us singing and bawling at the tops of our voices, louder and louder. About Hitler, who was to be hanged in his W.C. chain, and about Hamburg, Bremen, Rome and Berlin, already smouldering ruins to the slightly exalted eye—the whole repertory of scurrility, without the slightest regard for Gerda's presence.

Christian had probably imagined we should go for an evening stroll round the headland, and Jakob had quite certainly imagined we should play cards again, but neither intention came to anything. We sat where we were. A tremendous mutual sympathy, which included even the silent Kjeld, had been born as we sang. It held us close and prevented us from getting up. We perceived our union as happiness, and joyfully relived our joint achievements. As yet they didn't amount to much in fact, but in memory they did, and since even then they weren't glorious enough to satisfy our imaginations, we turned to the great and good deeds we were going to do hereafter. This was the best of worlds, after all. What did cares matter? Were they worth talking about, when one felt so heartily reconciled and linked with one and all at this table?

The sun vanished behind the woods on the headland before we had finished supper. The lake was tinged with mother of pearl, and long shadows began crawling up the ridge of hills to the south. Perhaps a lark was still singing in daylight high overhead, but we had no ears for it now.

Gerda went in to get a jacket, and brushed against my shoulder on her way back. Her mouth smiled as she looked at me, but her eyes were very dark.

Christian had moved his chair a little way from the table. He sat, pipe in hand, leaning back against the house and speculatively observing Jakob, who was just confiding to Kjeld where he meant to hit the first German he got in his sights.

'Now we want to hear something about Jakob,' Christian called out suddenly. 'He never normally says a word. Tell us something about the great crisis of your life when the road forked.'

'Hear, hear!' cried Leo. 'The chaplain's going to speak, the chaplain's going to give us a sermon. Now watch your step, it's not that sort of fork we want to hear about.'

Jakob hesitated a moment, looking at them suspiciously. He was sweating, and the short black lock dangled on his forehead. He had been taken by surprise.

'Jakob, what do you believe?' Christian went on unperturbed, reassuring him with a kindly glance.

'Well, chief, that reminds me,' Jakob spoke up at last, slowly and reflectively. 'I thought of something like that myself. I thought I'd propose a toast to you all. But instead I now move that we all propose a toast. *To ourselves!!*' he shouted all of a sudden, starting up like a jack-in-the-box and raising both arms in the air.

'I'm going to begin, I'm going to begin!' he yelled in consternation, to drown the laughter which had burst out and was threatening to drown his words for some time to come.

'Silence in church!' cried Leo, thumping a bottle on the table.

'Verily I say unto you that ye are troubled about many things,' began Jakob. 'But we read in the holy scriptures that everyone can be saved by his own faith.'

'We read what?' exclaimed Christian, taken aback.

'Quiet, you beer-dreg. Aren't I a divinity student? Oughtn't I to know what it says in the book of books? Therefore I repeat: Everyone is welcome to be saved by his own faith. For my part, I believe in Jakob. Implicitly. So I'm going to propose a toast to

100

Jakob. The fact is I think a lot of him, and in my opinion it should be a case of go and do thou likewise.'

'We do already,' we assured him in chorus.

'Today maybe you do,' he conceded. 'But not usually.'

There was a bellow of protest at the chaplain's scandalous discourse.

'I won't be interrupted now I *do* feel like saying something,' cried Jakob indignantly. 'You're all liars. *I* can see how you underrate me, and it gives me pain. It pains me very much. So much that I can't put up with it indefinitely. There's no saying how long I'll be with you. Here I stand humbly in my cups, knowing that when it comes to the point I'm much the most gifted of you all.'

Christian's pipe-smoke went the wrong way and set him coughing violently.

'Yes, and this is mainly for you, chief,' Jacob continued, eyeing him severely, 'for you think you're so damned clever, but I've taken your measure. I'd like you to get that into your head before you're too drunk to grasp it.'

'You're right, Jakob, you're absolutely right!' Christian had tears of mirth in his eyes.

'Of course I am,' said Jakob. 'Why, I can see it clearly when we're playing cards. A man's intelligence can be judged by his skill at cards. We're agreed on that, aren't we?'

'That's right. By his zeal at cards,' Christian assented.

'Good.' Jakob went ahead without noticing the dig. 'As I'm always the winner when we play cards, it follows that I have the clearest head. Furthermore'—he again had to raise his voice to obtain a hearing for his monstrous assertions—'furthermore, it's evident that I'm also the bravest of us. There's only one of you I'm really frightened of, and that's Holger. But that doesn't count. He's just a hooligan!' With a magnificent gesture, Jakob swept a half-full bottle from the table.

'Bravo, Jakob!' shrieked Kjeld. 'That's right. If you only knew how right!'

'Hold your tongue, boy,' said Jakob, 'while your elders are talking. It's the chief I'm speaking to. Now see here, Christian, you think you've always got to keep an eye on Leo and me or we'll get up to something. You'd much better keep it on Holger. There's no telling what he'll get up to. Now you know.'

'Stick to the point, Jakob,' I said, trying to catch his eye. 'You were to propose your own health, remember.'

Jakob swayed and had to lean against the table.

'Here's luck!' he exclaimed, seizing his lager. He emptied the bottle at a draught and tossed it over his shoulder. It landed a good way down the slope.

'Next!' prompted the eager Kjeld. 'It's going round, it's your turn now, Leo!'

But Jakob was far from finished.

'Sometimes I feel a queer craving,' he said pensively, and hiccuped. 'A craving for something to fill me. Fill me completely. So I won't vanish. That's it. Sometimes I feel so empty. In here.' He struck himself hard on the chest and produced another hiccup.

'There's always a cure for that.' Leo reached quickly across the table, seized the big bottle of schnapps and passed it to him. There were still four or five inches left at the bottom.

Jakob grabbed the bottle, and despite Christian's shout of warning he put it to his mouth and took three mighty gulps.

He stood for a moment with the empty bottle in his hand, breathless as though from a fierce fight; then he gave a gasp and let it fall. The alcohol started to his eyes as a sheen of lunacy. Bewildered, he spun round, but he couldn't see us, he couldn't see anything. He bent his knees and took off. In one tremendous bound he flung himself backwards over the edge of the hill.

If he had hit the steps leading down to the meadow, he might have broken his back. But Jakob didn't hit the steps. His life was evidently of some significance, for his giant frame landed in the big elder tree a few inches away from the steps, and the topmost branches caught in his pullover and held him up. There he hung for a moment as though crucified between heaven and earth, with outstretched arms and legs apart, before crashing slowly down through foliage and snapping twigs.

Almost unconscious, he let himself be hauled passively out of the tree when we regained our wits and came to the rescue. We carried him up the steps and placed him in the basket-chair. He was rather scratched about the arms and legs, and had a rent in his pullover, but otherwise he seemed none the worse for his flight through the air.

'Jakob!' Leo sang out, trying to make contact with him. 'Hi! Jakob!'

Jakob didn't stir, nor did his eyes open, but all the loving sympathy he felt for himself was in his voice, as all of a sudden he said thickly:

'Jakob's going to bed now. Mush shleep.'

'No, not yet Jakob, it's too early,' Leo remonstrated, holding a glass of beer under his nose.

Jakob sniffed warily. His nostrils twitched.

'Ugh!' he said. 'The whistling!'

'Where, Jakob? Whereabouts?'

'In the wood,' said Jakob.

'That wasn't a wood, Jakob, it was only an elder tree.'

'It's a pine wood,' maintained Jakob. 'I've got into a great, thick pine wood, and it's whistling. Ugh!'

He shook his head violently to get rid of the noise, and all at once his eyes opened. Leo got such a fright at this spectacle that he recoiled several steps, and in a twinkling Jakob was on his feet. Before we could stop him he seized his chair, lifted it high above his head, and hurled it down the slope. He flung himself on the next chair, tossed it the same way, and then went straight for the loaded table. But with that we were on top of him, holding on.

'You've got to make a strategic withdrawal, Jakob, do you hear me!' Christian shouted in his ear. 'That's an order. Do you understand!'

But Jakob was deaf and blind. Against his furious resistance and demented howling, we pulled, dragged and carried him round to the back of the house, meanwhile pounding away with might and main at his muscles with our clenched fists. Then Leo and I got a grip on his arms and went running and lurching to and fro across the grass to wear him down. He was unbelievably tough and strong, and we were completely exhausted by the time he calmed down enough for us to let go of him. Even then we weren't quite easy, till he had peaceably taken his stand behind a bush and made water until it frothed.

'Why, you piss like a horse, man!' Leo grunted appreciatively.

'What's that?' Jakob slowly turned his head, listening intently.

'You heard,' I said.

Leo had struck the right note. I had seen a gleam kindled in Jakob's eyes, he was himself again, and it was the good old chaplain who now threw his head back and laughed his noisy laugh.

'Why, that's just exactly what I do! Thank you for those few kind words!' he exulted, looking fondly down at the impressive symbol of his manhood.

But radiant with pride and self-satisfaction though he was, he had the greatest difficulty in holding himself up. We could do nothing with him, his eyelids were dropping all the time. When Leo offered to accompany him to bed, he accepted without more ado, and retired staggering, but in good order and with the honours of war. To be on the safe side I escorted them to the bedroom, and saw that they came to no harm while crawling on to the bunks and into their sleeping bags.

When I went out again it was quite dark, but the black August night was swarming with great stars, and the air was as still and mild as ever. Down in the meadow the grasshoppers were chirping.

Gerda sat smoking, with her legs tucked up beneath her. Each time she took a puff at the cigarette I saw a little of her face. The forehead, the cheeks, the lowered eyes. And her fingers.

Christian and Kjeld were having a subdued, sensible conversation about the war. About the conquest of France, which was now complete, about the Germans, who were withdrawing to the Rhine, and about the likelihood that soon it would be all over, so that one could get abroad.

Christian was doing most of the talking. Kjeld hardly spoke. In fact he hadn't said very much all day. He knew he couldn't catch the tone of Leo and Jakob, and had sense enough not to try. But even now that he had Christian to himself he didn't really open up. To him everything here was simply a waste of time—temporizing and delay. He bore with us patiently, and was always friendly and obliging to everyone. To everyone but me. Whenever he looked at me, which wasn't often, he had that obstinate, injured look on his face: those defiant, exultant eyes, which said: Just you wait, I'll make a fool of you after all!

Drunk as I was, it suddenly became crystal clear to me that he was firmly resolved to die. He would get himself shot down at the first opportunity, and there was nothing to be done about it. No matter how I kept watch, he'd give me the slip all right. That was the meaning of his expression, that was what the eyes said. It was my fault that he had nothing to live for, and now he would pay me out by dying. Then it would be up to me.

There was still plenty of schnapps left in the half-bottle, and I filled the glasses all round.

In the bunk-room Jakob flared up into a final neigh of laughter. It was the evening's witticism rising again in his fuddled consciousness.

'Do you three always go so hard at it, Holger?' asked Christian with a smile, though not without a little uneasiness at the thought of Jakob's attack.

'Naturally,' I said. 'Why not? Cheers.'

But now Christian had obviously had enough. He only pretended to drink. The glass came full from his lips, and he concealed it for a moment under the table-edge. When he put it down it was empty. He stretched in his chair with a deep yawn.

'Don't you think we should be turning in as well, dear?' he said, looking conjugally at his wife.

I hastened to fill his glass again, in spite of his ardent protests. I opened more beer, offered cigarettes and tobacco, asked if they were hungry, and before they could say anything bolted into the kitchen and set to work with the breadknife. We must get started afresh.

All at once Gerda was in the doorway. I didn't turn round, but I was aware of her scent and warmth just behind me.

104

'What's all the noise, and what are you doing that for? Nobody's hungry.'

'There's no sense in going to bed and packing it in already,' I said. 'If we eat a bit more we can stay up a long time yet.'

'We've just eaten all we could swallow,' laughed Gerda, stretching her bare, brown arms across the table and putting the bread away with sure movements.

'Make a cup of coffee, then. You're so good in a kitchen.'

'Do you think this is the time for me to be sober,' said Gerda, breathing hard.

'Gerda and Holger, what are you up to?' Christian called from outside.

'What do you think?' muttered Gerda. She leaned against the door-jamb and took a helpless little step into the next room.

'Come along, then, Christian!' I said jovially. 'We've damn well got to finish this! I hereby challenge you to a duel with the rest of the schnapps. You must flee or follow the custom of the country!'

Christian gave a deprecating laugh and held out a hand to Gerda.

'Aren't you cold?' he asked solicitously.

'No, I'm all right.' Gerda shook her head, not looking at the hand. 'But there's no reason why you shouldn't go in if you're sleepy. Give me another drink, Holger.'

'Very well, we'll keep it up till I fall off my chair,' said Christian desperately, lifting his glass. 'You're stark, staring, raving lunatics, the whole crew. It's a damned good thing I shan't have much more——' Then, to drown his slip of the tongue, he shouted, 'Well, here's luck!'

This time I made sure the schnapps went down his throat. He wouldn't empty any more glasses on the ground. I took a deep breath after drinking, and realized that I was good for plenty more; my capacity tonight was almost unlimited; though if I became as drunk as Christian would be in half an hour, I wouldn't get much joy either, out of being alone with Gerda. To be on the safe side I left the beer alone; it only made you sleepy. Christian obviously hadn't learnt that dodge. He washed his schnapps down carefully with beer to take away the taste. I knew I could keep drunkenness under if I gave my whole mind to it. I had done it in the past and I would do it again now, but while I was bracing myself to keep a cool head, I clean forgot to say anything. Of course I ought to have made some blithely casual remark. Through my dogged concentration I suddenly heard the infernal chant of the grasshoppers. And the silence, the silence.

Now no one at the table said a word. Kjeld, Christian and Gerda were all looking away from me, so far as I could distinguish their faces in the dark. All was silent as the grave, the grasshoppers were the very shrilling of silence, and I had no idea how long the silence had lasted. Had the world stopped? Or was I dead drunk after all? With a feeling of having revealed myself beyond recall, I began rooting frantically in my mind for something to say to them. Something trivial, the more trivial the better.

Suddenly Christian's voice came out of the dark. Dead tired, nerveless and despairing.

'It's too one-sided a match, Holger. With your physique you could drink an elephant under the table.'

'You just think too much, Christian. You've got too many brains,' I replied. 'It would do you good to be really knocked out for once.'

'What do you mean?'

'Ask Kjeld,' I said.

'No.' Christian got up with an effort. 'I'd rather take you on properly while I can still stand.'

Knowing that Christian was a ju-jitsu expert, I said, 'Show me some of your holds, I want to learn a bit.'

'Too dangerous at the moment.'

'That's a yarn. You needn't carry them through.'

Christian shook his head.

'We're too drunk, I say, and I might be tempted beyond my strength. Come on, fair and square.'

Christian's reach was as long as mine, but I was nearly a head taller. We began to wrestle amicably, or so it seemed. In actual fact Christian was straining every nerve to get a quick decision and possibly take me by surprise, while for the moment I stuck to passive resistance. He launched two attacks in vain, and then a third. The very instant I felt him giving up again and loosening his hold, I clamped down on him. He gave in the middle like a straw.

'Now stop, while all's well,' Gerda said warningly, ill at ease. 'I'd far rather you had a drinking-match.'

I held Christian up so that he wouldn't fall, and then let go of him. But he had no sooner found his feet than he made a lunge at me. I could see this was to be a regular ju-jitsu hold, and sprang back against the house to have the wall behind me. Then in a flash he was closing with me. I tore my left hand free and tried to get him by the scruff of the neck before it was too late, but as I drew my elbow back, my whole arm went through the window.

Bits of glass hailed down on us. Christian stopped at once, laughing hysterically, but Gerda jumped up with a scream.

'Take it easy,' I said, 'no harm done.'

106

For I felt nothing at that moment. But a moment later my arm was dark red and burning hot.

'Get indoors!' shouted Gerda, running on ahead for a candle.

We all trooped into the kitchen. Blood was pouring from the wounds, and they hurt sickeningly now.

'Better get a bucket,' I suggested rashly, though for ten seconds I had the same grim thought as the rest: it's the artery.

It wasn't. Christian made a hurried examination and found three long cuts, of which only one, near the wrist, was very deep or serious. He ordered me up on the kitchen table, and there I had to lie full-length while Gerda bandaged my arm with a couple of torn-up drying cloths.

'Damned if you don't look like a corpse, lying there with the candles at your head!' grinned Christian.

'Do be quiet, man!' said Gerda indignantly. 'It's no laughing matter.'

'What a shame we didn't need the ambulance, Holger,' said Kjeld. 'I'd have been glad to fetch it, you've so often done me a good turn.'

Gerda stopped work, and looked ready to kick him.

'No, no,' said Kjeld, 'you don't understand! I only meant I was so often in hot water when I was small, and then Holger always came to the rescue.'

'That's what you meant, is it?' said Gerda caustically.

Christian was intently following Gerda's every movement, and there was real meaning behind the facetious words when he said at last: 'Holger always has the luck! Look, Kjeld, how solicitous she is. She's never been like that with me. I'm heartily jealous, I can tell you!'

Still, there was a pleasant, forbearing atmosphere in the dim kitchen. Our binge had passed off at a stroke, we were feeling sober and relieved. And possibly rather foolish. Two of us anyway. Christian lit me a cigarette and went to have a look at Jakob and Leo.

'Would you mind getting the bottle of schnapps, Kjeld, if there's anything left in it,' I said. 'I could do with a small one now.'

Kjeld shook his head and went off.

Gerda took the cigarette out of my mouth, when we were alone together. She knocked the ash off into the sink and took a long, greedy pull. There was a fly buzzing high up in the window, behind the blackout curtain.

'Jakob's right,' she said. 'You *are* a hooligan.'

'Yes,' I said.

'You'll come to a bad end.'

'You too.'

She gave me back the cigarette and looked me steadily in the face.

'I love you,' she said.

'They're sleeping like little cherubs, those two,' Christian reported with satisfaction. 'And won't Holger be good and go to bed now?'

'If there's no more schnapps,' I said.

Kjeld came in and held up the empty bottle.

'There was a drop left,' he said, 'but I've just drunk that.'

'You poured it away, you mean,' said Gerda. 'Didn't it occur to you that he needed it?'

'Quite right, Kjeld!' laughed Christian. 'You're a peace-loving character, and we've all had enough, even Holger.'

They escorted me to bed. Gerda unrolled my sleeping-bag and took off my shoes.

'Isn't he going to get a kiss as well?' asked Christian.

'That'll be saved up,' Gerda replied. 'The patient shouldn't be excited at the wrong time. I thought you knew that.'

I lay awake and heard them clearing the table and taking in the chairs. When Kjeld came in I pretended to be asleep, and he crept noiselessly into bed. Soon after that Christian and Gerda went into the little room next door. There was only a thin partition-wall between, and I could hear everything they said. But they hardly spoke at all, and very soon their room fell silent. The last I heard before going to sleep was the shrill chirping of the grasshoppers down in the meadow.

10

At the beginning of September, after three informers had been liquidated in less than a week, the Germans imposed a ten-o'clock curfew, and the very evening it came into force our code turned up again in the London Broadcast. Message for Bacchus.

We made an early start, so as to be back in good time before curfew, but the railway area was swarming with sentries, and for once we really bungled the job.

It was a cold, windy evening with sudden heavy showers—starry one moment, overcast the next. We were seeing shadows and hearing noises at every turn, and several times we bolted for cover in a fright. After three vain attempts to get down on the line, Christian became nervous and called off the action on the grounds that it was too late to move farther away from the town and try somewhere else. Strictly speaking he was right, but it was certainly something of an anticlimax.

However, we were to find that Christian had a card up his sleeve. On the way home he took Leo and me into a pub and stood us a couple of beers, over which he proposed that we should wipe out this evening's ignominy by carrying out our first daylight action. Hitherto we had worked only in the evening and at night, but of course sooner or later, and preferably while we still had Christian as a leader, we must accustom ourselves to going out by day as well. The message from London was valid for twenty-four hours, so we naturally agreed at once, and it was arranged that on the afternoon of the next day we should ride south along the main road in quest of some spot where we would have the chance to do a really neat job of work undisturbed.

'If all goes well, I expect it's the last railway sabotage I'll be doing with you,' Christian concluded.

His words remained in the air, and a long, resigned silence followed them. That pause had its own little history.

Christian had been very pleased with the way we got together at the week-end, or so he said, and the day after the binge, when we were all lying in the tall grass of the meadow nursing our hangovers, he had thought the time ripe to reveal his decision to leave the group.

It was a lovely day. Tall towers of cloud were moving with majestic slowness across the sky, trailing broad belts of shadow behind them, which kept the great ridge to the south constantly changing, and the atmosphere couldn't have been better. It could have been a good deal better after his announcement, however, for Leo and Jakob rebelled immediately. When they realized that his decision was unalterable, they were for some minutes on the brink of mutiny, and Christian had to exert all his powers of persuasion and all his authority to bring them round. Then for no apparent reason—it was very marked and rather disturbing—Leo shut up and began to sulk.

He had been more or less surly and intractable ever since. Gradually I saw that only a real sacrifice would appease him. I made my choice and resolved to sacrifice Kjeld. He and Leo would never get on anyway. Accordingly I promised Leo that Kjeld should be transferred to another group as soon as possible. Christian could doubtless arrange it easily; or if his disappearing trick did cost him a bit of trouble, that was just too bad. I further promised the sulky Leo that Kjeld should if possible be replaced by Ejgil, of whom Leo thought highly. I had met Ejgil in the street one day, and he had told me that his mother had now calmed down to such an extent that he would certainly be able to join us soon.

The result was a distinct improvement in Leo's temper. But it couldn't make him forget his soreness at Christian's decision. Of course he realized that Christian could be even more useful higher up the ladder, and that he was almost too good for the rough work. All the same it was Christian who had enrolled us, Christian who had got things going at long last, and just as we were in the thick of everything and fancied all was in perfect order, he got tired of us and went away. Leo, in spite of his criticisms of Christian's arrangements (for we were always kept on a very tight rein), had placed enormous confidence in Christian as a person, and he now felt let down and rejected.

Moreover, though he said not a word about it, he must certainly have felt himself passed over in the choice of a new group leader: if Christian must and would go, then obviously there was only one person who could really take his place, and of course his name was Leo.

'We're too thick on the ground,' he began irritably, when we had said goodbye to Christian and were walking home together. 'That's why we get jumpy. Three's quite enough for the job.'

110

'Three?' I queried. 'You've always said four was right.'

'Well, now I think three,' he said pettishly. 'Anyway there's something wrong somewhere.'

I agreed that there had been too many of us this evening.

'But tomorrow we're sure to have work for five,' I said. 'And there's no knowing how often we'll be going out in daylight.'

'Always thinking of your sick auntie, aren't you!' snapped Leo. 'But if that fool Handsome puts a foot wrong——! Remember what you promised!'

'Very good, corporal!'

'Shut up,' said Leo.

'You know,' I said presently, 'Christian was right off his stroke this evening.'

'He's got wife-trouble, I shouldn't wonder,' Leo returned, drily. 'What do *you* think?'

'Shut up,' I said.

'Very good, sir!' grinned Leo.

And so we parted.

At four on the following afternoon we set out, dressed as hikers, with shorts and rucksacks, and saddle-bags on our bikes. Leo, Kjeld and I went on ahead in search of the ideal spot. Christian and Jakob were to start fifteen minutes later with the explosives

The weather was still chilly and drear. Like the previous evening. Admittedly it was no longer raining, and the wind had dropped, but it wasn't what one thinks of as a September day. The sky was ashen with low, hurrying clouds, and everything looked ravaged and washed out after the night's storm.

In the chestnut avenue just before the viaduct a troop of boys were throwing stones and sticks up into the trees. The ground was a mass of thick, spiky shells; they lay on the road in hundreds, yellow outside, pure white within where the glossy fruit had been hidden. The fallen leaves that had come down with the spoil were sticking to the wet asphalt and making the road greasy and slippery. Autumn, autumn.

The viaduct itself was under close guard, and there were still more soldiers patrolling the track below. It was not a very hopeful prospect, but we comforted ourselves with the thought that it must soon improve.

A little farther on we began sizing up the situation more exactly. We made detours down the side streets, trying out all the good places we knew and several untried ones, but with the same result every time: sentries everywhere, and too many of them at that. They were lined up at intervals of two hundred yards wherever we could get a view of the track. This was something unusual. Off-hand, we might have thought they were expecting the Führer in person, but Christian had told us before we set out that last night there had been innumerable explosions on the north-south line. The saboteurs had been out all over Jutland, and this morning all normal train services were suspended. So it was on us that the soldiers had to keep watch, more particularly now while the system was being repaired. It was an honour we could have done without. We gave up, as we were intended to do, and followed the road till it was quite clear of the suburbs.

Now we were out in open country, and I must admit I felt a lot safer here than in the densely built-up areas we had just left, this being daylight sabotage, and not an ordinary night-manœuvre in which we were protected by the dark. Moreover, here the guards were father apart. On the other hand the track was now so high and exposed that we couldn't reach it without being visible a long way off to anyone on the road.

So on we went. We had never had to go so far afield, and by now Leo was in a flaming temper. The thick red vein in his forehead had begun to swell, and he didn't answer when I spoke to him.

'Now listen, Leo,' I tried afresh. 'Don't you think we——'

'No, I bloody well don't,' snapped Leo.

'We're getting too far away. It won't do. We shan't be able to get back.'

'Nothing's happened yet, has it? Nothing's ever happened when I've been on the job.'

'No, and that's just why——'

'We can send baby home, if it's him you're so worried about,' hissed Leo.

Then at last we struck lucky. A mile south of Hojby Hill there was a bit of woodland, just where the road approached the railway again. To make it quite perfect, the line curved gently at the far end of the wood. If we placed the bombs there, on the inside of the curve, the sentries would have to be pretty close before spotting us.

If there were any sentries. We hadn't seen any on the last stretch, but that might be accidental. I sent Kjeld back to direct Christian and Jakob, telling him to keep a good lookout on the way. Leo stopped and dismounted. Wheeling his bicycle into the wood, he stuck it behind a pile of logs and devoted himself to a closer study of the curve. Meanwhile I continued on the short run to Nyvang Station.

When I returned, Leo was sitting behind the woodpile inhaling a cigarette. He had simmered down, and was quite calm now.

His nervous irritability was gone. I had often seen Leo worked up, but never nervous as he had been earlier when we couldn't tell where we stood.

'It's a cinch,' he said complacently, smiling at me. 'Now the others can get here as quick as they like.'

'They can wait a bit if they like,' I replied, sitting down beside him. 'There are two sentries just coming up from Nyvang.'

'Were there Germans in the village as well?'

'Not that I could see. But I met a porter at the station, and he told me that off and on they have some quartered on the farms round here, though he hadn't heard of any at the moment.'

'Then where the devil have they come from—the ones you've just seen?'

'From Hojby, naturally. Where else? They've a big barracks at the station, you know. That's where all the sentries come from.'

'Oh yes, that's right.' Leo pinched out his cigarette and put the stub away in the matchbox. 'Well, we can just wait till they've passed. There's plenty of time.'

Presently Kjeld and Jakob arrived, and a bit farther down the road we could see Christian toiling along. Kjeld and Jakob had also seen two guards, which meant that just then there were four Germans approaching the wood, two from each side, north and south.

'Oh God, I'll never do that again!' groaned Christian, dropping down behind the woodpile.

He was completely exhausted by the ride, and for a few minutes couldn't speak. This wasn't the easy, superior Christian who usually led us into action, but then it wasn't the ride alone that had winded him. I could tell by his face that he hadn't slept last night. Every feature was blurred by a subtle weariness, and it cost him a visible effort to pull himself together.

'The guards aren't the worst part, gentlemen,' he said at last, putting to an end discussion in the ranks. 'To hell with them. The worst part will be getting away from here. We're too far from the town, there are five of us on bicycles on an open road swarming with Teutons the whole way, and for the first two hours it won't even be getting dark.'

Jakob made his joke for the hundred and seventeenth time.

'Is there any reason why we shouldn't take the train back?' he asked with a poker face. 'Just for once!'

We had laughed at it the first twenty times, and we laughed again now. At him. Because he still thought it so wildly funny.

'We needn't go back the same way,' I put in. 'We could go on to Nyvang and west along the by-roads. Then we'd come out on the Silkeborg road. But it means a pretty big detour.'

'Do you know the way?' asked Christian.

113

'Yes. And there are no Germans in Nyvang.'

'Are you sure?'

'Yes.'

'Then we'll do that,' Christian decided.

'The guards'll meet in the wood here before long,' said Leo. 'That may be quite useful. In any case aren't they just the relief taking over?'

'That's what *I* thought,' replied Christian. 'The two we saw were walking so purposefully. But don't let's count on it.'

'Does it really matter what they're up to?' I asked. 'We can just wait till they've gone their different ways. Once we're down in the curve they won't be able to see us anyway, not even from a hundred yards off—will they, Leo?'

Leo shook his head, but Christian looked at me as though he hadn't quite grasped what I said.

'No, of course not,' he said at last. 'Well, Leo, shall we get ready?'

Christian and Leo went a little deeper into the wood, behind the next woodpile, to unpack their things. Kjeld remained sitting by the road in case of accidents—there were quite a few cars going by—and Jakob and I went to opposite ends of the wood to keep watch on the German sentries.

I got as close to the track as I dared before lying down on the wet ground. The cover was splendid. If only the trees wouldn't sigh and tremble and drip so damned mournfully whenever a breeze went through their branches. Just in front of me a fine, symmetrical little maple gleamed sorrowfully, its big leaves already quite yellow. Those outspread hands seemed to be saying: Look, I'm ready; what's to come is only winter and death after all; patience is all one needs.

I felt a gust of mortality and gentle resignation wafted from that tree; and from the others, though their leaves were still brown; from the forest-floor and from the heavy blackness of the lately ploughed field beyond. A gust of death. Not the sudden harsh, annihilating death we had brought with us, but a slow, more gracious death which was not our portion. Death in another world, within a cycle in which we had no part. In which mankind had no part.

From the edge of the wood, where I was lying, I had a view of the whole countryside. Close to the railway stood a farm, but there were no signs of life there. Nor anywhere else. Far away in a hollow there was still a trail of dank, rainy mist. Everything was bleakly forlorn and desolate.

Sure enough, the two sentries whom Christian, Jakob and Kjeld had seen came trudging purposefully from the north down

114

towards the wood. A long-legged gangling fellow and a little middle-aged, middle-class one. Not exactly picked men, by the look of them. As they drew nearer I could make out their expressions as well. The tall one was bending forward, holding his arm sideways across the small one in a parrying gesture, as though to prevent his escape from the stream of talk which he continually directed at him, and all the while eagerly scanning the little man's face for signs of approval.

The little man just plodded on, unapproachable and arrogant: out of temper with his mate and with everything and everyone else in the world, but particularly with the Wehrmacht, which had dragged him from the watchmaker's shop at home to this wretched country and forced him to waste his valuable time doing sentry-go on these idiotic rails: when he might have been sitting in the back shop brushing up his German poets and philosophers!

Now they were so near that I could hear the tall one laughing at his own jokes. He had a laugh like a door creaking. The little man didn't laugh. He stuck his broad, plump jowl in the air, closing his eyes behind their horn-rimmed glasses like a toad.

They passed the place where I lay, and the little man was almost hidden by the railway bank. I could only see his steel helmet sticking up as they went by.

About half-way between Jakob and me and just short of the curve where we meant to place the charges, they met the guards from Nyvang. And now the gangling windbag found a better audience. Indefatigably he trotted out the story about their *Feldwebel* or *Gefreiter* all over again, waving his arms about like one inspired. Before long the newcomers were in roars of laughter. How on earth would he ever bring himself to abandon such a receptive audience? It certainly came hard, and when he did reluctantly tear himself away from his comrades, the little man had long since lost patience and was walking off to the south, while the pair from Nyvang began to approach us in their turn. Evidently it *was* a change of guard. At any rate I had now seen enough, and fell cautiously back to Christian and Leo.

They had the whole works all but ready. Twelve charges altogether, six for each track, were to be fixed to the rails and connected by the fast-burning white Cordtex fuse, so that they should all go off at once. The charges were packed, the fuses joined up and calculated, nothing remained but the little detonators and the actual explosive pencils which were to send everything sky-high.

'What about the ignition-time, Leo?' asked Christian. 'Five minutes, or ten?'

'I've got some of each,' Leo replied. 'Let's say five. Then at least there's no fear they'll be spotted, and we won't be more than a few seconds getting to Nyvang once we're through.'

'Better say ten,' decided Christian. 'After all there are twelve charges to fix.'

I beckoned Kjeld up, showed him where I'd been lying and told him to go and give us a sign when the Germans were a hundred yards from the wood.

'Those are the two that have just been relieved,' I added. 'They're going off duty, so at any rate there'll be nothing from that quarter. We'll get down to the line as soon as you and Jakob give us the signal, and you'll see for yourself when we're finished.'

Kjeld listened attentively, but without looking at me and with downcast eyes. Leo glanced after him sarcastically. He had something spiteful on the tip of his tongue, but it had to stay there, for just then a little stick hit the woodpile, thrown by Jakob, who had come a bit nearer and was now nodding zealously and waving us towards the track. A moment later Kjeld was at his post and giving the signal from his side.

'Here, Leo! Wait a second. What are you doing with the pencils?' exclaimed Christian. 'Don't press them yet!'

'Why not? We always do it before we go down,' Leo said cocksurely.

'Always! I know we have, the last time or two, but today we'll wait. To be on the safe side. Right?'

'Hell, I've just done it,' grinned Leo. 'What can it matter? You getting worried about your pension? We've got ten minutes yet.'

'Oh well, let's get it over.' All the same, Christian was upset and angry. 'It's unforgivably rash to press the pencils before the charges are fixed. Remember that when you're on your own,' he admonished. 'Why, it goes without saying!'

We made quickly for the line. I was a few steps ahead, and on reaching the wire fence I leaned out and looked both ways. The track was clear, of course. Hell, we were clever! If we hadn't the art of sabotage, who had?

Before helping Christian and Leo over the fence, I gave a final glance up towards Kjeld. All was well there. And down towards Jakob.

Was I seeing things? My scalp prickled and I wouldn't for worlds have believed my own eyes. But it was true! Jakob was waving desperately, with every sign of consternation on his long face. Get back! Away from the fence!

We made straight for cover, and the explanation appeared soon enough. It was the young, long-legged German. He came bounding back along the sleepers, straight towards us. Already he was abreast of Jakob, and Jakob was doing nothing to stop him. Of course he and Kjeld both knew that of late we had been rash enough to press the pencils before fixing the charges because everything always went so smoothly for us, but he couldn't be certain we had done so today, on our first daylight job; and besides, what was he to do if he wasn't to fire and alarm the other sentries?

The situation was paralysing.

Leo swore his deepest oaths when the German began shouting and whistling after his two departing comrades. Whatever the gangling idiot might be in need of, or had forgotten with all his blasted chatter—perhaps only a match for a furtive smoke on duty—here we sat with twelve nice pink marzipan pigs in our laps, done up in ribbons and bows and stuffed with almonds and all. Help yourselves, please! For in ten minutes they would explode. In less than ten minutes. In nine minutes. Perhaps in eight and a half. I looked at my watch. What the hell were we to do? I looked at Leo and Christian and got no answer. Their faces registered indecision and desperation and nothing else.

'You see!' Christian breathed panic-stricken, white in the face.

'We've got to go down. Now. I daren't wait any longer,' stammered Leo. He had hardly any voice.

'We can cover you with the tommy-guns,' I tried to say, feeling in my pocket. Yes. I had remembered a spare magazine.

The German was abreast of Kjeld, and now he slowed down a bit. He whistled and shouted again. So his comrades still hadn't heard him.

Then suddenly there was the snap of a branch on the forest floor, and the fence wire in front of us moved and squeaked at the joints.

What now? Was it Kjeld? Or Jakob? I half rose. It was Kjeld. I saw him run down the bank and leap up on the rails behind the tall German. Unarmed. He meant to throttle him. Steal up and throttle him from behind, overpower him with his bare hands. But he tripped over the sleepers, and the German heard and turned like a flash. That same instant Kjeld closed with him.

I didn't see what was happening in the next few seconds, I was on my way over the fence to Kjeld. But as I slid down the bank there were two shots and Kjeld tumbled backwards into the ditch. The German stood with his rifle on his arm, gaping after him.

Then I fired. I let off half the tommy-gun's magazine, and the young German stiffened and dropped his rifle. He threw his head back convulsively and clutched at his throat. Then he fell over on his side.

Now there were shots from the other side. The grumpy little

117

man was letting fly at Christian and Leo, who were already up on the rails, busy securing the explosive charges.

Where on earth had Jakob got to?

'Halt, halt!' bellowed the German, as he ran towards us.

I had no chance of hitting him with a tommy-gun, he was too far away, but I tried all the same, since Jakob was doing nothing. I took careful aim with the tommy-gun against my cheek, and emptied the magazine in small bursts. The little man stood still and aimed his rifle at me.

'Jakob! You blasted idiot!' I shrieked hysterically, throwing myself into the ditch. 'Shoot him, can't you!'

And now, at last, Jakob woke up! The drum-revolver banged twice. The little German doubled up and fell forwards. He crouched on all fours, groping and trying to reach his gun. Then Jakob was on him, firing again.

I turned to run towards Kjeld, but just then I heard someone crying out and calling me. Christian. Christian had been hit and lay moaning on the rails.

'Get him away!' shouted Leo. 'I'll finish this. But for Christ's sake mind the fuses!'

I lifted Christian as best I could, and straddled my way over rails and fuses and charges, down into the ditch with him.

Now Jakob was beside me to lend a hand.

'No! Get along to Kjeld, he's lying in the ditch, and bring him back!'

'Hurry for God's sake, before it all goes sky-high!' groaned Christian.

I gripped him under the armpits, dragged him up the bank, and with great difficulty got him through the fence and into the wood. He could no nothing to help himself, and groaned piteously at the rough handling he got.

Then there was more shooting. Evidently the two sentries who were going off duty had returned.

Now where was Jakob? Why didn't he fire at them and keep them off? I left Christian lying, and loaded up with the spare magazine. But Leo—Leo was wonderful. He had finished, and was throwing himself safe and sound over the fence and head first into the wood.

'Where's he hit?'

'In the hand and the knee,' Christian answered for himself. 'And in the foot. I can't stand up.'

'Run down to the road and stop the first car!' I said 'Otherwise we've had it, we'll never get out of here.'

Leo snatched my tommy-gun and rushed for the road. And at last, at last we heard Jakob's revolver again. So the guards must be quite close.

'Hurry! Hurry!' begged Christian. 'Take me on your back, I can hold you round the neck with my good arm.'

I got him on my back and lurched off with him through the wood for all I was worth, tripping over branches and roots at every step. We had just reached the woodpile—when the first explosion came. I flung myself on my face, and the battered Christian went flying over my head.

'Ah, that's so soothing!' groaned Christian. 'Come again! Mine too!'

And Christian's bombs went off with a fresh boom.

'There, no farther now. Just leave me here.'

'Keep quiet and help a bit,' I said, starting to grapple with him again. But now he fought against it and made himself stiff and heavy.

'Listen. There's a car!'

We paused to listen, and could distinctly hear the sound of a car approaching from the south. It slowed down as it entered the wood. But it wasn't drawing up! It was going by! Why hadn't Leo stopped it?

'No, no, I've had enough, leave me here. I'll never be fit again. I'll never operate again with this hand!'

'Shut up! Come on, pull yourself together a bit! You mustn't give up like this,' I said fiercely.

'Oh, my hand, my hand! It hurts so. I can't bear it. And my foot! I knew things were going to go wrong.'

'Oh, for God's sake shut up!' I said desperately. 'Think of Gerda!'

'I am!' wailed Christian. 'I am thinking of you and Gerda. I think of you all the time!'

'What the flaming hell's bitten you now!' I shrieked, beside myself.

'I can lie here and hold up the Germans while you get away!'

I was on the point of hitting him, but there were tears of pain and despair in his eyes, and I took him under the arms again and dragged and carried him along, cursing him steadily.

'Do you think we want you lying here being a hero and playing Hemingway!'

'You devil, you devil!' sobbed Christian. 'If you knew what you've done to me, and if you realized what you're doing now!'

Then I heard a car again, and now a brake, and Leo hallooing. It was too good to be true. Hysterical joy rose in my throat, for it *was*. true. I could see for myself now. Leo had stopped a wretched, splendid little market-gardener's lorry coming from Nyvang. When I got Christian down to the road Leo was standing on the running-board, and the driver, a big, dung-stained gipsy fellow with a cap and a black moustache, was just turning round. I took in the puddle at the roadside, by the grass verge:

119

Leo had been vomiting with fright—so that was why the first car hadn't stopped. Then the driver got out, and of his own accord helped us to get Christian in the back.

'I don't mind driving you,' he said to Leo. 'Can I? Can I drive myself?'

'Not bloody likely!' said Leo.

'But I'll get the lorry back? If I don't get it I'm ruined.'

'Of course you'll get it back! It'll be in the market-place in an hour's time with a can of petrol on the front seat. Is the tank full?'

'Full right up. I filled it just now as I was starting.'

'Then beat it. The Germans may be here in a minute!'

Jakob came charging through the wood, wildly waving his revolver.

'I heard the car and I thought you were going to leave me behind,' he babbled, distraught and gasping for breath, 'but I got one of them, the other one dodged and ran when the bombs went off, the revolver's no good out here, and I nearly got hit myself.'

'Where's Kjeld?' I shouted, grabbing hold of him.

'I moved him into the wood, and emptied his pockets.'

'What do you mean? Why didn't you bring him down?'

Jakob looked past me in silence.

'Why not? Answer me!' I shook him.

'He's dead, Holger.'

'You're lying, you rat!' I yelled. 'All right, I'll get him myself.'

But Jakob and Leo flung themselves upon me and held on.

'Why man, didn't you see? Didn't you see he fired right into his chest, twice?' Jakob shrieked hysterically. 'And now the Germans are coming!'

'The Germans! One wretched sentry!'

'One sentry! The farm was cram full of them!'

'What farm?'

'The one in the dip,' snapped Jakob. 'There's a farm there with its chimney smoking like a factory! I suppose you didn't see that either! You're a fine group-leader, it's all your fault. Listen for yourself! Here they come! Now can you hear them?'

And it was true enough. Excited shouts and words of command could be heard across the fields.

'Then we'll drive like hell!' cried Leo, jumping for the lorry.

Jakob followed him into the driver's seat. At the last second, when the lorry was already moving, I dived in over the tail-board and scrambled over to Christian.

Off we raced. In no time we were at Nyvang and out on the bye-road going west. There was no pursuit. The Germans hadn't seen us at all. We were concealed by the wood and then by the village on that tricky first stretch.

Leo was a very good driver, but of course he was going flat out, and we got a nasty jolting on the rough, stony road. I tried to make things a little more comfortable for Christian. We had laid him flat and covered him with our pullovers and a couple of sacks we found in the lorry, but in spite of them he was shivering. The wounds on his leg had long since bled through his shorts, and his hand was a clot of blood, but there was nothing I could do. I had no bandages.

I raised his leg slightly, propping it on one of the low boxes, and took his head on my lap. He was quite calm now, said nothing, and had stopped moaning. He lay with his eyes shut all the time, chilly and very pale. I thought his pulse felt weaker and weaker, and perhaps a little quicker than normal.

Once only throughout the drive did he open his eyes and try to look at me.

'That was stupid of you, Holger. You should just have left me. Now I'll make a fool of you after all, but it's your own doing.'

If the Germans had given the alarm at once—and the shooting of three sentries might well have galvanized them—there was a chance that the Gestapo would have had time to close the main approaches to the town. I considered how I might arrange the boxes on the lorry to camouflage us a little better, but I gave it up again and sat still. Christian was now fairly comfortable and dozing, and if we did run into the Gestapo, it would make no odds. It would be all up with us anyway.

But nothing happened. Leo avoided all main roads and busy streets, and we slipped into the town without being noticed. He drew up in a side street near Alykkevej, and Jakob jumped out and asked whether he shouldn't go and ring Frederiksen at the hospital to let him know we were bringing Christian. I agreed.

Jakob handed up the things he had taken from Kjeld's pockets.

'Don't be angry with me,' he pleaded. 'Of course we ought to have brought him home, I know that, but what was I to do? I couldn't do anything else. I got such a fright when all those Germans came over the dip, and I thought you were going to leave me behind. And he was dead all right! I swear he was dead!'

'Yes,' I said. 'Sorry.'

When we pulled up outside the casualty ward, the lovable, golden-hearted doctor was standing at the entrance, and didn't need many words.

'Has he fainted?' he asked, feeling Christian's pulse.

'Not quite. Are we home now?' Christian opened his eyes, smiling faintly at the sight of his friend.

Frederiksen snorted gently and said 'Hm' to himself. 'So they didn't see you?' he said.

121

'No.

'Then just make yourselves scarce.'

'Will he be safe here with you?' said Leo.

'Should be.'

'Do you think it's bad?' Leo asked, when the porters had taken Christian in.

'Quite possibly. It looks rather bad. But I can't tell yet.'

'I'll go straight down to Gerda,' I said. 'To his wife.'

'Yes, do,' said Frederiksen, as he followed the stretcher. 'But keep away, both of you. I'll be sure to ring this evening.'

Did he know anything? Did he know too?

'Here, put that on!' said Leo, handing me Jakob's pullover. 'You can't walk through the town in that shirt.' He was already behind the wheel. 'So long, see you later!' And he was gone.

11

THE tension of the drive and the speed with which everything had happened still urged me on now that I was alone, and I continued to act mechanically. I started to run down the drive that crossed the grounds between the staff quarters, but I hadn't run very far when I got a violent stitch in my side, and when I stopped and stood still my legs buckled under me and I almost fell. I continued at a walk, taking short, quick steps to get rid of the stitch.

With this slower movement the power of thought returned and at last I calmed down enough to realize that the danger was past, and that here I was, alive and unhurt and safely over the disaster in which Kjeld had lost his life and Christian perhaps his health and strength.

The realization brought a sense of emptiness. All at once the whole thing was infinitely far back in time and seemed completely unreal—those five dark figures running about the wood, making signs to one another, squabbling, shouting, shooting.

I became aware that I was shivering and icy cold from my ride at the back of the open lorry, and I found to my surprise that I had Jakob's pullover under my arm—wherever that had come from, and wherever my own had gone to.

I heard Leo's words—'You can't walk through the town like that!'—and now I grasped their meaning. I glanced down and saw the dark red, clotted blood on my shirt. I hurriedly put on Jakob's pullover.

From that moment the extent of the calamity began to register. The inner paralysis wore off, and feeling slowly returned. As the events became more real, my horror at what had happened grew and grew. All the panic I had kept down while the action lasted now surged up in me and gathered in my chest. My heart tried vainly to leap into my mouth. Terror had already clutched and pierced it like a claw. I whirled round, expecting to see my death catching up with me from a German gun-barrel.

There was no one behind me. No one in the hospital drive. Nor in the avenue outside, which I had just reached. I was all alone. But there was a dripping silence like that of the wood this afternoon. A sucking desolation, as on the black fields. Clammy fog drifted with the dusk under the street lamps, the trees stood motionless and impassive along the pavement. There was not a sound in the world. Yes! A big leaf snapped off and fell to the pavement. Here too there were chestnut trees. And at the corner the tram clattered its way to the city centre, screeching, like a madman, on the curve. I took a deep breath and began to run.

To Gerda. Gerda. Desire for her started up in me like the last vital instinct, and I ran as though it were still possible to run away and hide and forget. Still possible to attain the heart's desire and be happy.

After the trip to Silkeborg it had been harder for us to meet. We had had to be very careful. Christian had taken to checking up on the telephone, asking anxiously how she was, and twice he had returned from the hospital unexpectedly in the middle of his duty period on the pretext of having forgotten something. The second time, I heard his voice in the hall just as I was going to ring. I managed to go down in the lift and hide in a doorway across the street till I saw him leave the house. And then how greedily Gerda and I had fallen into each other's arms!

But now who stood in our way, who saw us now? No one in the whole world. Except one. The one who was chasing me as I ran and would soon catch up with me in the form of a certainty, a knowledge, permeating nerve and bone. But until then there was an evening, a night, an hour, half an hour.

The lift was in use and I didn't stop to wait for it. I ran up the stairs three at a time and rang the bell.

Her heels. Her light step in the hall. And there she stood in the doorway, Gerda, my Gerda, living and warm and near, smiling her happiness, looking straight past me to see if there was anyone else or if I was alone, and then turning back to me and realizing my state for the first time.

The expectancy and the smile vanished from her face. Her glance became uncertain, wide with inquiry; she stepped back, clasped her hands before her and wrung them in dismay. Still holding her gaze, I went in with her, pushing the door to behind me with my elbow.

Her eyes grew dark with knowledge. Dread and desire shot up in them like flames; again, again, that cruel awareness, as though life itself were running out, that bottomless depth of terror and despair and wild desire looked out at me.

When I put my arm round her shoulders, she yielded at once and came passively towards me, hiding her face.

My temples throbbed, and the blood was dancing before my eyes after that wild race; we stood clinging together in the dark hall without a word, and behind us lay the empty flat, the living-room, the bedroom.

I laid my hand on her forehead, bending her head back. She raised her face, eyes closed. Ah, that burningly sorrowful, insatiable mouth. Those unresisting, sensual lips, parted in rapture. More plainly than ever before they betrayed her one weakness. But the moment I touched and kissed them, I was lost. Her being opened to embrace me, and I sank deep, deep into her, and in that instant I knew what death was, and what Kjeld had felt when the bullets struck him.

Beyond terror and lust a sun arose in my heart and in seconds there was nothing but light, bright golden, heavenly light. Then it turned white and glowing and began to revolve, round and round, faster and faster. It grew and spread out from my heart in ever-widening circles, till my whole body and everything in me was burnt and destroyed in intolerable whiteness and glow.

When I reopened my eyes I didn't know where I was, and would have fallen if Gerda hadn't supported me. Then I felt her lips against my ear and heard her dark voice: 'You mustn't speak now, not a word.'

She put her arms round my neck and pressed her body against me, and I could feel her warmth everywhere, but it could no longer reach me. It was too late, too late. Too late for all eternity. Even as we stood there in the hall, everything started up again. The whole afternoon was repeated, clearly and inexorably.

The viaduct, the road, the maple tree in the wood, the rainy mist over the hollow, the mist which was smoke from a farm-house full of Germans, it's all your fault, and are the rest of us to be shot down now because you've no eyes in your head and walk straight into a death-trap?

'Gerda, Gerda, I love you, I love you,' I whispered desperately, pressing my hands against her shoulder-blades.

She broke away and took my hand. She led the way into the dark living-room, led me to the divan and pulled me down on top of her. I undid her dress at the neck, turned it back and kissed her bare shoulders. Her body followed the movements of my hand, and she was only waiting for me to tear the clothes off her and come.

It was no good, it was useless. The memories wouldn't stop. I was lying behind the woodpile with Christian and Leo, we got up, we went over to the fence, and the stupid tall German came bounding down the track, just to get a light for his cigarette. Kjeld ran on to the line, tripped over the sleepers, and suddenly fell backwards into the ditch. Didn't you see what happened, man? He fired right into his chest, twice, his clothes were all black with powder, it wasn't a pretty sight. And now the German stiffened and dropped his gun on the rails and clutched his throat and went down like a log.

'I love you, I love you, Gerda, Gerda help me, help me!' I implored, and I tore at her dress and burrowed down into her darkness, for I wouldn't see it, I would not.

But it went on. There was no oblivion left in the world. I kept on remembering, kept on seeing it again. The little German was taking aim at me, but Jakob had realized it at last, or had he been waiting all along for the German to get close enough and just let him fire away at Christian? Five yards off now, the little man fell on all fours and lost his glasses, and crouched there groping, half blind and screwing up his eyes, with the puzzled look on his haughty face of one who has just awakened, when he discovered that he hadn't just hurt his knee yet didn't see how it could be true, how it could happen to him. But Jakob had seen only too clearly. The German turned his head and looked at him in terror as he came rushing down the bank, and Jakob put that horrible monstrous pistol to the back of his head and fired, and the shot crashed into the brain, demolishing it to the bare walls. And now there was someone moaning and calling my name. Christian, the same Christian who came towards me one day here, in this flat, and took the pipe from his mouth and roared with laughter. And Hurry, hurry, hurry for God's sake, he said, before it all goes sky-high, but next moment his face twisted and all the other faces in the roar of an explosion, and I found myself shaking in every limb.

'Gerda!' I groaned, 'it's too late, it's impossible, I can't, we can't do it!'

She put her hand over my mouth, but I kissed the palm and took it away and pleaded again.

'Gerda, we mustn't, for our love's sake!'

'Darling boy, be quiet!'

'No, help me, stop me, stop me destroying everything, you've got to know what's happened!'

'I do know, and it's all the same.'

'No, you don't know.'

'Then I don't want to know, not now.'

'Yes, you must! Christian isn't dead, he's only wounded, Frederiksen's got him at the hospital. It's Kjeld who's dead.'

When I had said it she lay still in my arms, and I kissed her hands, put them over my face and kept them there.

Presently I found she was crying. I put my hands on her burning cheeks and kissed her eyes again and again.

'You mustn't cry, it isn't certain that it's serious, he's sure to——'

She burst into an agony of tears and said vehemently, 'It's not *him* I'm crying for, it's us!'

'Hush, my own one, you mustn't be so harsh now.'

'Not now, no! But in general I'm welcome to be, aren't I? In general you don't mind a bit. Oh God, as if there were any difference between then and now.'

'There is a difference! If you knew how——'

'There's no difference. Am I to listen to you lecturing me on harshness, when you're the most brutal man on earth? You come and take me with your cruel eyes, and then you won't have me after all!'

'I couldn't help it, beloved, I couldn't bear it alone. You must understand that, you must!'

'Oh my dear, forgive me, I'm sorry, I didn't mean it! I know you had to tell me, but why must everything be so hellish, why, why? Now it'll never come right for us, never as long as we live. I know that. Oh, if only I'd told him everything the other day as I'd made up my mind to.'

Her distress was terrible, and I couldn't bear to hear it. I tried to comfort her and make her be quiet, but she was beyond comfort.

'Why isn't he either dead or safe. He doesn't need *me* in particular, he could have so many others. Now I'll have to stay with him always. Oh God, I know it, I know it already, yet what am I to do? I can never forget you or stop loving you as long as I live.'

She broke down again in a rending, terrible fit of crying, and could say no more. I could find no words, and we lay there a long, long time side by side.

It was quite dark now, and I saw only the outline of her face. There was an intoxicating scent from her hair, and I put my lips against it and drew her closer. When she finally stopped crying, her tears ceased as abruptly as they had begun. She shivered, and gave an almost childlike sigh. Then her breathing grew deep and calm, as though she were asleep.

There was no noise from the harbour or the street, not a sound from any of the flats in the big building around us, the world was quiet again. Not as it had been earlier, when terror had clawed me. This silence was alive, a strong, calm force which pervaded me, concentrating and channelling my emotion in one direction: towards her.

I ran my hands through her hair and clasped them behind her head. I touched her eyes and her mouth and cheeks, recognizing feature by feature in the darkness the face I had loved, as it seemed, always and for ever. And a boundless gentleness such as my life had not held before was in her hand, in her fingers, which now awoke and began to move hesitantly over my face, caressing me constantly, loving and tireless.

I kissed her again. Her mouth no longer burned, and slowly

light dawned in my heart. Gone were the blind, anonymous urges of war, the harried autumn dark became quiet, grey rain, steady and tender as in spring. The cloud-ceiling broke up and parted, it grew lighter still, and the rain stopped. I was walking for the first time alone with Gerda in a place I ought to know well. The wind felt warm and round and almost palpable when I turned my palm towards it; it played in her dark-brown hair as we walked, brushing it back from her ears, and I took firm hold of her wrist.

Now I knew where we were. We were walking in the meadows. There were flowers everywhere: coltsfoot, pilewort, buttercups and dandelions were growing in the long grass by the brook, with a host of others she knew as well and could name. And they were all yellow.

Everything on earth was yellow, and everything above was growing bluer and bluer. Suddenly the great clouds had massed, blue-black, blue-grey and white; the heavens were full of them when we looked up, and imperceptibly they began their journey seaward in the soft westerly breeze.

And farther away still, far out over the meadows, the wild sunshine suddenly broke through the clouds, a column of light slanting like a ladder from earth to heaven.

In the late evening we were roused by the telephone. Gerda had taken the call before I was properly awake. It was Frederiksen.

They had operated on Christian as soon as he was brought in, and extracted three bullets. There was hardly any damage to the knee; the bullet had gone through the lowest part of the thigh muscle. The foot wasn't so good; one of the tarsal bones had been shot up and smashed to pieces; the joint could hardly fail to be stiff. And in his hand, his right hand, two knuckles were broken. He would never hold a surgeon's knife again.

Before leaving the flat we went through Christian's belongings and removed everything that might convey a suspicion of underground activity. We found some cartridges, one or two copies of *Free Denmark* and that was all, and we reached the hospital before curfew. Frederiksen had said we could stay the night there if we liked, and thus it was that Gerda was sitting by her husband when he came out of the anaesthetic and asked for her.

12

'I AM so sorry that I wasn't here!' said Ingerlise.

She had had the nerve to call on me now that I was back again in my own room: light and cool, with her shining fair hair in a new style. It hung long and drooping, nearly to her shoulders, framing the delicate oval of her face in a soft and charming fall. An angel hair-style, in other words. Ingerlise certainly didn't lack tact.

'Of course you know Kjeld and I were friends,' she said by way of preface, sitting down on the edge of my easy chair. 'But unfortunately I had no chance of a real talk with him towards the end of his life. Indeed, to tell the truth I hardly saw him, for you see in August I was away on holiday, and now I am sorry that I wasn't here.'

'The end was certainly quite something,' I said affably, 'so I can quite imagine how you feel.'

I gave her the story. Without extenuating circumstances. Yes, yes, she said several times while I was telling it, as though to defend herself.

'Yes,' she said again with downcast eyes when I had finished. 'And what did you do with—I mean—what about his—well, about his——'

'His body? The Gestapo couldn't identify it. And when the Red Cross inquired about him, they said they knew nothing of the matter.'

'Did his parents apply?'

'We asked them not to do anything.'

'I see.' Ingerlise nodded, shifting nervously in her chair. 'Why, exactly?'

'Why? Because what's done is done, and because we can't risk having the whole sabotage organization disrupted just when it's got going. Because the Gestapo might see fit to liquidate them or blow their house up as a reprisal—likely as not, the way they're behaving just now. There were plenty of reasons, as they very well understood.'

'Did you go out there to tell them?'

'The Red Cross went the same evening. I've been away till now.' After a pause I added, 'But we have an idea where he's buried, and one day he'll be found all right.'

The affronted, haughty expression she always wore with me—as though to be treated with anything short of fawning adoration were an insult and an encroachment on her personality—had yielded to something forlorn and wistful, which seemed genuine and made her empty dead face slightly more alive. The social climber in her did not seem so obvious as formerly, and her mouth just then was so defenceless and weak that I almost felt sorry for her. Puny and insignificant, there she sat on the edge of my chair—one who hadn't been equal to what was required of her. But had I?

'I thought perhaps you and Kjeld had discussed things at the end,' said Ingerlise.

'No, we didn't, I'm afraid. He must have turned against me.'

'I see. But what impression did he give? Did he say nothing about—I mean, did you have no conversation at all?'

'Practically none. I wasn't in his confidence any more, so now I've really nothing to tell you.'

Good lord, why should I pass on the parting words she was fishing for? There was no forgiveness or healing in them, quite the reverse, and it could only make her more unhappy to learn that Kjeld had seen through her. And if there was something in her after all, if she had really been hit by Kjeld's death, was there anything that I of all people could say?

'Oh,' said Ingerlise pensively, and again, 'Oh.' It struck her as rather odd all the same, that I should know nothing whatever. 'Haven't you been out to see his parents?' she asked. 'I think you could do that much at least!'

Of course I'd been. Long ago. But what took place in the yellow villa on that occasion wasn't for anyone else, and least of all Ingerlise. She and that house had nothing to do with each other.

'I'll make a point of going out there in a day or two,' I said.

'And none too soon, either. It's over a fortnight now.'

Her tone had changed, and there was some of the old smug assurance in her voice as she underlined the gravity of my omission. This was how I knew her best.

'Do you remember the Christmas party at the Beach Tavern last year?' she asked.

'Very well indeed.'

'I told you then I was afraid you weren't a true friend to

Kjeld and that you'd do him harm. I just don't believe you understood him. Did you know, for instance, that he wanted to be a poet? Or rather that he was a poet?'

'I had no idea,' I exclaimed in surprise. 'I never heard about that. It sounds very interesting.'

'I thought he wouldn't have told you,' said Ingerlise complacently. Then she checked herself. 'Not that I know all that much about it, but he must have felt he could trust me, for several times he read bits aloud to me. They were awfully good. Very beautiful and poetic. And I rather think that at the end he was gaining a fresh understanding. Of suffering.'

'Do tell me how,' I said, 'I'm interested. That's a subject I'd like to know about.'

'You must excuse me,' Ingerlise said lightly. She put out her little hand and ostentatiously straightened the books on my modest shelves. 'He didn't say much about his experiences, you know. And besides, it's not something to be spoken of lightly.'

'No, of course not,' I said apologetically, aghast. Did it never occur to such people that they themselves might be fathomed and seen through?

'I feel it's so unjust that he of all people had to die. When he was so handsome, and so clever and talented.' When I did not reply she said, 'Don't you think so?'

'Oh, absolutely! Beyond a doubt,' I said earnestly. 'It's as though people like him didn't quite come into the same category as the rest of us.'

I got up and went over to the window, where I stood with my back to her.

'I'm glad you can recognize and admit that at last,' Ingerlise said. 'And I quite understand how it must upset you to know he was a poet. If you hadn't led him into that sabotage of yours, he would certainly have done something great.'

Now she had me! At last, at last, she'd cornered me for the knockout. Now she would get her own back. Revenge is sweet.

'Don't you think some of his things might be published after the war?' she went on. 'Of course I know he was too young to have completed anything, but anyone who can read would see how talented he was. The very incompleteness would emphasize the sadness of his early death. If his diary and letters were included, there would surely be enough for a book. As it happens I have several letters from him that could be used. But I suppose I'd better discuss that with his parents,' she answered herself, when I kept my mouth shut. 'Of course you aren't much interested in that kind of thing.'

'I understand it even less,' I said. 'You go and see them, they've a great regard for you.' Next time, I thought, next time!

Ingerlise paused. Was she really going to be content with that? Hardly. A short step farther ought to be safe enough.

'There ought to be one person at least to remember him as he was,' she challenged, giving my books another little pat. 'He shan't vanish without trace, I'll see to that.'

'It's kind of you to take charge of his reputation,' I said, and with that I faced her at last. 'Very kind and very unselfish. But do you really think you'll have time?'

'What do you mean?' Ingerlise looked me defiantly in the face.

'To a lady like you he can hardly have been more than a puppy. Oughtn't you to be seeking out more mature company instead?'

Ingerlise not only turned scarlet, her face went to pieces. She was so indecently out of countenance that I had to turn back to the window to give her a chance to arrange her expression.

For a good many seconds there was silence behind me. Then she tried to speak. I could hear the attempt, but it was no more than a hysterical little gasp that escaped against her will, and she gave up. She rose hurriedly and collected her things. Only as she stood in the doorway did her full heart run over.

'You ought to be struck dead!' she hissed in her small voice. 'I wish it was you that was dead!'

The door slammed behind her, and she was gone.

When Christian was moved from hospital and installed in a country parsonage, Leo, Jakob and I had no hand in it; and of course Gerda went along to look after him. The idea was to dispatch them to Sweden by the underground route from Sæby as soon as Christian could stand the journey. Frederiksen told me this briefly, but when I tried to find out when they were leaving he said he didn't know, it certainly wouldn't be just yet, and added that I mustn't think of getting in touch with them.

For all that, Gerda's letter was no surprise. I had been expecting to hear from her. I felt sure she wouldn't leave the country without saying goodbye to me. The letter had come from Ålborg, where she and Christian were now, and where they would have to wait at least a couple of days before moving on. Would I meet her there?

I got her letter at midday, caught the train she had suggested, and sat with my heart in my mouth the whole way, for fear the line would be sabotaged and I'd be too late.

Gerda was at the station to meet me. I caught sight of her from the carriage window as we pulled in. She was walking up and down the platform in a brand-new grey coat and skirt, a black alpine cap and black gloves. Assured and smart, with a wholly new poise about her. Suddenly sophisticated and suddenly quite invincible. There wasn't a grain of weakness in this lady, she was invulnerable and proudly superior from top to toe. No disguise could have been more effective. That I should ever have dared to love her was dizzy presumption, and that she should have rejected all others to fall for me, an impossible idea.

It wasn't quite so impossible when I was standing before her. She put her arms round my neck and kissed me openly, just as though she were my wife and I her lawful husband, home from a short business trip.

We walked out into the strange town arm in arm. The sun hadn't shown itself all day, and though it was only four o'clock, darkness was already descending from the low, hurrying clouds. The October air was cold and raw, but it was pure, untinged by the melancholy decaying autumn of woods and gardens. The whining wind for ever blowing through the streets of this exposed town came straight off the harbour, from the North Sea's winter-grey, restless swell. Now and then there was a harsh, driving shower of heavy rain that soon penetrated one's clothes.

We walked like a nice married couple for the length of a street. Then I drew her into a gateway, and the old madness began again. As before, everything was only hunger and thirst for her. What had happened to Christian and Kjeld hadn't happened, there was no reality but the body's craving. She was meant for me and she remained my girl. I had her still, I still had her and could forget that soon all would be over. Yet again and again it burst upon both of us at the same moment that this was the irrevocable last meeting, the hail and farewell for ever, and we clung together wildly, as though we could still halt the inevitable which would take our birthright from us.

We went down streets and alleys we didn't know, and over a long bridge. We crossed squares and thoroughfares we had never seen before and did not see now. Everywhere we sought out the darkest corners, lurking in cellar-mouths and doorways and on staircases, till someone disturbed us and put on the light. Every moment when I wasn't kissing her wet, full mouth and touching her burning throat and her cheeks was a moment lost.

We ought to have discussed things, but I kept on postponing it. Why talk when there was so little time, and what was the good of talk? The only thing that was any good was being close together. As long as we did not draw apart, it was still possible to forget what was in store and blunt the pain lying in ambush.

And yet it was not possible. It wasn't the same. I could hold her when I pleased, but there wasn't the same glow in her now, she wasn't carried away as I was. There was reserve in her yielding, forbearance and pity at the heart of her embrace, where once there had been only heedless unashamed desire. She

133

was another's now. I could sense it and it was no delusion. The fight was lost.

'I promised Christian you'd come out and say goodbye to him,' she said, at length. And those were the first words to pass between us that day.

'Then he knows I'm here?'

'Yes.'

'Does he know all the rest?'

'Yes. But he still wanted to see you.'

'Why?'

'So that you won't think he bears you a grudge. And *I* couldn't even ask him to forgive me,' she added, looking away.

'What did you say when you told him?'

'That I'd stay with him if he wished it.'

'And he?'

'Nothing. He just accepted.'

We found a respectable beer-cellar near the harbour and went in. It was quite a small place with a bar in the middle, but there was a billiards-room at the rear, where a couple of workmen were enjoying a peaceful battle and a chat with the waitress, who sat by keeping the score. The subdued, soothing noise of the balls as they knocked into each other and overturned the pins on the dark green cloth came to us all the time. We settled down in the far corner and ordered beer.

Gerda had been carrying her gloves and cap the whole way; now she put them down on the table. She dried the rain from her cheeks with my handkerchief and shook out her hair. Her dark brown hair. Again I had been thinking of it as black, though it was really just a very dark brown. There were no drops winking in it this time, it was only shining and sleek with rain.

'Lend me your comb too,' she smiled. 'I must look frightful.'

'As usual. Still it suits you to be a little thinner, unless it's just that coat and skirt.'

'The same to you. You've positively faded away. You're even losing your hair. You're already getting thin on top, you poor lad. You might at least have waited till I'd gone.'

'This is how I've always looked,' I said. 'It's Christian who has hair right down on his forehead.'

'Nonsense,' said Gerda, reddening. 'He's fair and you're dark, that's all the difference.'

'Oh,' I said. Then I said, 'If you want to be a real lady, you'll have to put your hat on again. And your gloves.'

'And keep off the beer, too, I suppose. Well, cheers.' She put her elbows on the table and drank. 'With all our faults, you wouldn't really say we've gone in for hard drinking?'

'No, we must have a good deal in hand,' I said.

'Then why not start with a schnapps to warm us up?'

I saw how gravity and strength had pervaded her being and made her tranquil. Beautiful and gentle she sat facing me, with her pure, well-marked features and her soothing grey eyes. All the bravado and aggressiveness had gone, and now the only childish thing in her face was the firm roundness of her cheeks.

Violent and passionate as everything had been between us, at that moment, after my utter solitude for the past fortnight, I saw our whole relationship in the same matter-of-fact light that Gerda now radiated, and realized how much at home with each other we had been from the outset. I had never had to dance attendance on her or keep her amused or wonder what impression I was making on her. There was nothing coquettish or challenging about her, she didn't give you an enhanced, fidgety awareness of your own ego, like the girl who only feels she exists when she can use her partner as a looking-glass. Gerda was there with her own warmth, independent and straightforward, like no one else I had ever known, and her presence made me free. I wasn't alone. I no longer had to bear everything by myself.

Gerda asked about Kjeld. I told her what little I knew, and it wasn't news to her. Frederiksen had naturally kept her and Christian informed.

'I know I'm a party to his death,' I said. 'There's no getting round it.'

'I imagined you would say that,' said Gerda. She was sitting with her elbows on the table, propping her head in her hands as she did so often. 'But do you really think he would have blamed you for his death?'

'He was terribly bitter against me those last few weeks. He wouldn't even talk to me.'

'In that case——!' Gerda shrugged her shoulders, and moved her glass to get the beer spinning round. 'Would you or I ever saddle anyone else with our mistakes and misfortunes in life? You know we wouldn't.'

'Can we be so sure of that, if we think about it?'

'Yes, perfectly sure.'

'We're so damned tough.'

'Yes we are. But when you come down to it, Kjeld's death had nothing to do with anything or anybody but himself and his own destiny.'

'I'd rather think of it as a sacrifice,' I said. 'When I remember his last action, that seems fair enough.'

'It looked like a sacrifice, I agree. But suppose it really sprang from bravado and bitterness and not from faith or friendship? I doubt if Kjeld had any desire to live.'

'He was the happiest, gayest person imaginable till he got that notion about poetry. The real Kjeld might have sacrificed himself in just that way, but for love. In fact it would have been very like him. He must have grown out of all those other ideas and come to himself again. Don't you think?'

'I don't know, Holger. Of course you tried to bring him to reason.'

'That's not the word. I didn't advise him, I deliberately wrecked a chance for him. But never mind about that. I did it because I thought I was doing right and I won't go back on it. My one mistake was in not refusing when he wanted to join the group. Then I gave in to the spoilt child.'

'By that time he was determined to die somehow. The war was only a pretext.'

'Perhaps. But I just lost my head. Our relationship hindered me from seeing the whole picture, and I was too stupid to distinguish between his need and my own.'

'Or perhaps it was that Kjeld was too weak.'

'There's weakness in most people. And at times there's an urge to destruction in us all. More or less. Who can claim to be immune?'

'And in an artist the urge to destruction will inevitably get the upper hand if his talent's not great enough. I'm quoting my husband, please note,' Gerda smiled. 'We've discussed this as well. And Christian says that if you imagine an artist without his creative powers, there's nothing left but an urge to destruction. He used those very words.'

'He's damned clever,' I said. 'But tell me what you do about conscience, once it's roused.'

'Holger, look at me. You have made me human again by using those very same tactics. I told you last summer in the woods that you'd made me alive and warm again, and it was true. Thanks to you all my aggressiveness and absurdity disappeared. I'd lost faith in love, and what is a woman without that? You gave me back my faith without knowing what you gave, without even meaning to give. I know we've behaved like a couple of criminals—I'm afraid it took no less than that with me. But the crime isn't the only thing, there's more than that— and it won't end that way. It is your strength that is in me now. You, and no one else, have made me strong enough to leave you and remain with Christian, as I know I must, without becoming what I was when you first met me.'

Strong enough to leave you, as I know I must. To leave you and remain with Christian, as I know I must. Without becoming what I was when you first met me. Suddenly I realized. Even though I already knew it was over, though I had felt ten minutes ago in the street that she had ceased to be mine, and felt it beyond all forgetting, only when I heard it from her own mouth, spoken so levelly and courageously, did it fully dawn on me that I was to part from her.

I should never again hear her coming along the passage to my dark, miserable room, and see her walk in, warm and out of breath from the stairs. She would never again touch my things and lie down in my bed. We should never go out into the world together and wake one morning high up in the mountains. We should ripen and grow old separately—if we did grow old. She would bear children that were not mine, and teach them to love another father ; her living hand, lying here on the table, would grow wrinkled and slack without my seeing it; her figure stoop and her cheeks grow cold when I was not there. The whole of lovely life would pass over us as we lived sundered, and it was now, on this October evening and in this windswept alien town, that I was to let her go.

For a moment I thought desperately: we know, we know which emotion is the strongest, even if lust itself can sometimes be put aside. Can duty itself be a lust, another, deeper lust? And is there a mystery in what they call renunciation?

Never in this world. That was senseless rant, something that had its place only in castrato singing and 'art'!

Here she sat, the girl among thousands who was meant for me, my girl, my destiny, my life. There was no doubt of it. I had only to look up to see that it was true. Was I to submit, then? Was I to accept her leaving me? It was out of the question. Desire for her rose in me afresh. It surged up as raging pride and defiance, and the whole dream of her and my future was present in me as I lifted my head and looked at her to impose my will.

She faced me bravely and steadily across the table. Her eyes shone with a gentleness, with a lustre and depth they had never held before, and which was only for me. All we had had together was alive in them, but not as passion and open flame—as past happiness and pain. She was beyond it now. It was all transmuted into purity and serene will, into a clear, strong knowledge.

The waitress crossed the room with a beer for the man in the opposite corner. The coins chinked in her apron pocket as she felt in it for change. From the back room there came again the sound of the billiards balls clicking on the green cloth and knocking down a couple of pins.

Gerda's gaze didn't falter. I couldn't call the dizziness and weakness into her eyes, couldn't light the dark, burning passion in them, couldn't reach her any more. She halted me, she willed this parting, and she was the stronger.

I wasn't knocked out. No such luck. With my whole consciousness I had to see and understand that she was no longer mine and that I had lost. I felt it as a physical pain that brought tears to my eyes, and I couldn't take it. I laid my head on my arms, hid my face from her and gave up.

Everything else I could have borne: fear of death, sabotage and war, Christian's misfortune and Kjeld's death, in which I had some part; but I could not bear to part from Gerda. I couldn't bear to have my birthright taken from me. That was too much.

'I don't know how else I can help you,' Gerda said quietly. 'You're only too inhumanly strong. Last time we were together, you were much wiser. Then your body knew it all.'

She ran her hand through my hair. Like my mother hundreds of years ago. And like a tide of warmth and gentleness her dark voice went on, giving me sadly and proudly what she was still free to give.

'Ah, my dear, I'm so unspeakably thankful that you exist and that I've known you. That life should be just as great and terrible and good as I thought when I was seventeen. I'll never again go against it or complain of anything. And I don't insist on having you to keep. That would be too much, surely, if the whole pattern's to be spun? But think of those who don't see the whole pattern. Who have always to do without the one they could love, who wait year after year and at last forget what for. We at least have had it, we know that it exists, and that after all you can only be really happy with one person. And we know that you can choose to be unhappy, because friendship also exists. But then, perhaps love and friendship always go together.'

I couldn't answer her, and I couldn't feel anything except that my life was over because she was leaving me. There was no more to lose and no more to hope. I knew now that I wouldn't survive the war. It was not possible to survive. If I didn't get shot I should be worn out when it was over. With Gerda I might perhaps have come through; alone I could not. But then perhaps one didn't make a really good saboteur till one had realized that there was no life beyond and that there was never meant to be a continuation. It wasn't only the risk and the struggle one had to accept, it was death. What came after was not for me and my kind.

'I know you can take it without growing bitter,' said Gerda. 'And I am sure you won't give way to temptation, as Kjeld did.

You're not going to court disaster or run amok because you can't have your own way. I know that, Holger, I'm convinced of it! There'll always be something in you that you can't escape.'

'What else can I do but offer my services? Go back and go on. Act as though I still believed in it all.'

'What do you believe in, if not in this very thing we're doing voluntarily for Christian?' she said, laying her hands on mine. 'If there had been no war we'd just have left him, without thinking of anything but ourselves. Now we act differently. We must. And at bottom it's not because he was wounded so terribly, but because we choose this way.'

All about us the world was the same as before, things were taking their normal course. The pub, as usual at this hour, was filling up with workmen and clerks who had just knocked off and meant to celebrate with a turn at billiards and as many beers as they could afford in one evening. Life was going on, good-humoured and equable, with its repetitions and small compromises. A possible life, in which one rubbed along somehow, had good times in company and bad times alone. A hard life, in which one would slowly and patiently be worn down, resign oneself and learn to make do. Such a life as I should some day be living. Perhaps. At half strength. Free of the high seriousness and tension in which the war and Gerda had plunged me. Partly retired. As life accepted such men it would also accept me if I settled down at last, offer me gladly its everyday concessions and give me what I needed to exist. No more and no less.

Before we got up to leave, Gerda said:

'There's only one course for us, Holger. Even if we should be disappointed, even if we can't have our own way, we must never grow bitter and never bargain with life. We've no right; no one has; it's not decent.'

The place where Christian and Gerda were staying till they could move north again was an ordinary red brick villa on the edge of the town. The proprietor, an old merchant who had got rid of his business some years ago, lived all alone in the roomy house now that his wife was dead.

The sitting-room Gerda led me into was crammed with furniture—heavy upholstered armchairs and shiny mahogany. On the floor lay a carpet an inch thick, and wherever it was possible to put anything, on the sideboard, cabinet, piano, and on all the tables, large or small, there were crochet table-centres, crystal vases, silver cups and china animals, together with half a century of family portraits, glazed and framed, and in most cases nearly covered up by amateur photographs of more recent vintage tucked into the edges of the frames.

Above the sofa, which was the size of an Indian elephant and much the same colour, hung an oil-painting to end all others: Denmark's spreading beech woods on the Baltic coast. The sunset gold ran out over the glassy water like a fried egg.

Under this idyllic show-piece sat Christian with his injured leg on a stool and a big white plaster bandage on his right hand. The active, energetic Christian was out of the game. But not broken or tormented, as I had dreaded. Not at all. He looked cheerful, almost gay, and was obviously moved to see me. Perhaps all the more because he felt helpless, and couldn't get up when I held out my hand.

'Leo and Jakob send their regards,' I said.

'Thank you. So they know you're up here?'

'I managed to let them know before taking off. I couldn't just leave them in the air, if anything should happen tonight.'

'No, indeed!' laughed Christian. 'It'll do you good to see what responsibility feels like. Have you a job to control them?'

'Not a bit. How could I have? Don't you know we're the smartest group in the town—and the best trained?'

'Thanks. But in general, how are you all doing? Everything as it should be?'

'Jakob's voluntarily abandoned his drum-revolver for a tommy-gun. He's not going to risk the magazine jamming again.'

'I don't understand how it did.' Christian suddenly turned grave. 'It's not possible, it just can't happen, you know. But we were lucky that day, we were indeed. Tell me, how's Leo getting on?'

'Always griping that we're short of a man. He thinks after all that we're too few now. It was better when there were four of us.'

'Just what I expected.' Christian laughed again. 'And so you are too few. Four would be better. But then you'll easily get a new man now.'

'We don't want anyone else. Not just yet.'

'How about Ejgil?'

'That's different. We'd be glad of him. But he's rather hanging fire.'

That was as far as we got, and we had no chance to say more to each other. The hall stairs creaked under a heavy tread, the door opened, and our host came shuffling into the room and put a stop to conversation.

He was a hunched, grizzled man with melancholy brown eyes and a huge hanging jaw, which had held a short curly pipe with a bright metal band round it for the last generation. He gave me a curt nod in passing, but otherwise took my presence as a matter of course, and without a word of inquiry headed straight for the deep armchair beside Christian. Snugly installed, with his big, idle toil-worn hands at rest on the shiny arms of the chair, he took over and began to entertain us. Or rather went on entertaining. He resumed the—as I gathered from Christian's dumb-show—endless monologue on his own life which only necessity had induced him to discontinue. Dogged and deliberate, now and then puffing at his pipe, which he rather surprisingly managed to keep going as he talked, and inexhaustibly patient with himself and his slow-functioning and at times wholly failing memory.

He had got to his military service, to the very moment when after two re-shoots with the 381 he had been elected marksman of his company, and everything that I heard him relate was by way of a sequel and dealt with weapons and military associations. The soldiers' club of the Sixth Regiment, of which he had now been a member for forty-eight years, the Society of Danish Brothers-in-Arms, of which he had lately become an honorary member, the Frontier Association, in which he had served a term on the committee, and so on and so on. The local rifle club, with its annual clay pigeon shoot, dwindled by comparison, to a detail worth mentioning but of no great moment.

The old merchant was completely lost in these recollections of his splendid youth and prime, here and in other towns farther south in Jutland, which had quite possibly shown a more patriotic temper and keener appreciation of a life's effort in the service of the country. He addressed no one in particular, not even Christian. He didn't wait for an answer, didn't even require one as long as we were there, and for that matter he could equally well have told his story to one of the china dogs.

Christian, who had begun by saying yes and no politely in the right places, made one serious attempt to derail him. That was when we were to be informed of the exact placing and individual scores at the jubilee shooting-match of the Brothers-in-Arms in 1927. The figures really seemed to have escaped our host's memory for good and all, and quite a long pause ensued, which Christian had the bad taste to take advantage of.

The old merchant turned his head and looked mournfully at him, with big heavy eyes which were all but rolling out of their sockets. He did not heed the interruption. Instead the lost figures suddenly came back to him. He turned his head back again, once more gazing before him with a remote look that saw nothing of the present, and pursued his course.

I sat looking at Christian and Gerda. Or as often as I dared, and when they weren't looking at me. I noted how much had changed between them, and how right their relationship seemed.

141

He needed her now, couldn't go on hiding it, and indeed was making no secret of it. Not once did I see his eyelids twitch. And the way Gerda moved about him, her care and frankness, showed me that these two were now at one. For the first time it was possible to regard them as a pair.

The merchant ground on. He obviously wouldn't break off his story, let alone move from his chair, while he had us in the room. We weren't going to be left to ourselves. But perhaps it was a very good thing after all. In a sense it was a relief that he sat there maundering. What should we have said or done without him, in the long run? We couldn't all burst into tears and fall on one another's necks.

When the mahogany clock on the table-centre on the mahogany sideboard struck eight lingering, golden and melodious strokes, I determined to leave, though there was still an hour and a half before my train. But as well now as later. Why put it off? It wouldn't get any easier in the meantime. On the contrary, the more I thought about it the more difficult it would get. Everything was settled, all that remained was to get up and go.

Gerda took a packet of cigarettes from her bag and offered them to Christian and me. She gave us a light as well. It was a new box, and the scrape of the match on the strip of sandpaper sounded unnaturally loud. Soon the three cigarettes were smoked out.

I got damnable palpitations as the cigarettes grew shorter, and I found that I couldn't make my body move. At the last moment I tried to lash myself with my own weakness, but self-contempt had absolutely no edge. I was still sitting there when Christian, the last of us, crushed out his stub in the ash-tray. I'd have to set a fresh deadline. Five minutes by the mahogany clock. Down to the quarter-hour.

When the gilded hand reached the top of the figure three and the five minutes were all but gone, I got up, went out into the hall and put on my coat. I didn't button it. I went back into the room and sat down on the edge of Christian's footstool. It wasn't me and yet it was. I knew what I was doing and yet I could do it.

Gerda got a shock when she saw me with my coat on. She hadn't expected me to go so early. Her breast rose, and she held her breath. I didn't look at her eyes, I didn't dare look higher than her throat where the heart was beating. Nor did I shake hands with either of them. But I met Christian's clear gaze and saw that all was understood between us. He nodded imperceptibly.

'Just sit where you are. I'll let myself out,' I said.

The old merchant turned his head and peered after me as I went. Without a trace of surprise. He was sucking tenaciously

142

at his pipe to make it draw properly. Before I had reached the door I heard his voice grinding on.

I opened the front door cautiously and shut it behind me without a sound. For a moment I could see nothing whatever, so black was the outer darkness. I felt a tightening of the chest that stopped my breath, but it wasn't tears. It didn't come from within, but from without. It was the October night itself, starless and impenetrable, confronting me like a wall. Not till I was going down the steps did I feel the wind, and the thick, incessant drizzle from the North Sea.

PARRISH

The Novel by Mildred Savage

A mighty and violent novel set in the tobacco planta-
tions of Connecticut, this book deals with the clamorous
pressures of modern industry conflicting with deep-
rooted family traditions. The battle is symbolised in
the personal feud between Judd Raike, the all-con-
suming tyrant and land baron, and the 19-year-old
newcomer to the plantation, Parrish MacLean.

5s. 0d.

Ace Books